MORE THAN EXES

Also by Elizabeth Briggs

More Than Music
More Than Comics

MORE THAN EXES

A CHASING THE DREAM STORY

ELIZABETH BRIGGS

Cover Designed by Najla Qamber Designs
Model Photo by Lindee Robinson Photography
Models: Anthony Hamlin and Kelly Kirstein

ISBN (paperback) 1502473437
ISBN-13 978-1502473431
ISBN (ebook) 9780991569618

www.elizabethbriggs.net

For Gary
My favorite good guy

CHAPTER ONE

If there was one thing I'd learned, it was that good guys never got the girl. Even if the good guy was covered in tattoos and piercings and wore an old Joy Division shirt with the sleeves cut off. Nope, the ladies would still recognize him (or in this case, me) for what he was and ditch him for the guy who practically screamed, *I'll break your heart.* Usually that guy was my brother, Jared.

My Saturday night had just begun, and I'd already had the lesson drilled into my head. We'd unloaded all our gear and stashed it backstage but had hours to spare before we were scheduled to go on. It seemed pointless to arrive at the club so early, but the organizers of the UCLA vs. USC Battle of the Bands had told us to show up at 6:30 PM, and Jared would sooner slit his wrists than be late.

With so much downtime before our 10:30 PM set, I headed for the bar to grab us a couple of beers. On the Rocks was a small club in Hollywood that held a few hundred people. The place was almost empty now, but we were the last band to perform and I figured it would fill up by then. The few who'd arrived early stood around in the big, dark room either at the bar along the back wall or in front of the small stage where the first band was setting up. I didn't recognize them, so they must have been from USC.

At the bar, a girl with a red plastic cup in each hand nearly crashed into me. She took a quick step back, but one of the drinks slipped from her grasp. I managed to catch it without even a spill. Not bad, if I said so myself.

"Wow, great save," she said, taking the drink from me. "Thanks."

"No problem. Sorry I almost knocked you over."

"Totally my fault." She looked me up and down, checking out the ink on my arms. "Hey, you look familiar."

The girl was hot, with bleached hair and a low-cut, black dress showing off a small butterfly tattoo between her breasts. Definitely my type. I didn't want to get too excited, but damn, it had been way too long since I'd gotten laid. Or gone out with anyone. Tonight might finally be my lucky night.

"Do you go to UCLA?" I asked. I didn't recognize her, but it was a pretty safe bet most people at the show either went to my school or to our rival. "Maybe we have a class together."

"I do." She cocked her head and studied me again. "Are you in Villain Complex?"

A fan of the band? This was getting better and better. "Yeah. I play keyboard."

"That's how I know you!" She laughed a little, and her chest bounced, making it look like the butterfly was flapping its wings. *Must not stare, must not stare.* "I saw you play last week at that parking lot show. You guys were amazing! I went home and bought all your songs from your website."

"Thanks." I offered her my hand and smiled. "My name's Kyle, by the way."

She juggled the drinks into one hand and slipped the other into mine. "Tiffany."

She liked our band, she seemed interested in me, but now what? I couldn't offer to buy her a drink since she had two already. Why did she have two? Was she going to meet someone? No, she was giving off that single vibe so probably here with a friend. I needed to make a move but had to keep it cool, too. *Think, think, think.* Man, I sucked at this pick-up-line stuff. Oh, I could ask her about her major. That was always a pretty safe bet.

Before I got the chance, she asked, "So I guess you know Jared Cross?"

And just like that, any hope I had of getting some action suffered a swift and violent death. *Womp womp.* "Yeah. He's my brother."

"Really?" She glanced around, like she hoped Jared would pop out from behind me. I could tell the second she saw him because her breath got fluttery and her cheeks turned pink. What was he doing? Serenading random strangers with his shirt off? It wouldn't be the first time.

I turned and spotted him leaning against the wall, talking to our drummer, Hector. Not half-naked, thank god, but even fully clothed Jared had this crazy effect on women. As if to prove my point, he looked over and gave us that lazy smile that girls could never resist. And then, to top it off, he winked.

I hated it when he winked.

I rolled my eyes and turned back to Tiffany, but she was a goner already. She made a little sound like a gasp, and her eyes flitted back to me. "Could you introduce me?"

I should have seen this coming. Why would I think she would ever be interested in me when my stupid brother was only feet away? I didn't get it. We shared a lot of the same DNA, but I must have been missing the "come-hither" gene. Even though Jared looked like a toned-down version of me—fewer tattoos, natural hair color, and no piercings—girls somehow had this radar that honed in on him. It's like as soon as they heard him sing they decided, *Yes, this guy is trouble. I must go after him.* And they all thought they could fix him, like they'd be the one girl who could make him settle down and change his ways.

Keep dreaming, ladies. I guaranteed that tomorrow morning I'd be patting Tiffany—or some other girl—on the back as I walked her to her car and wished her a nice life. Jared didn't do relationships, and no girl was going to "fix" him because he wasn't broken. He just liked women. Lots of women. All the time.

Like I said: good guys never got the girl.

I'd already lost Tiffany's interest. No point in continuing with this. I led her over to Jared, who raised his eyebrows at us, and Hector, who shook his head like he knew where this was going already.

"Jared, this is Tiffany. She's a fan of the band and wanted to meet you." My voice sounded flat, but then, I'd given this speech quite a few times before.

My brother flashed that same annoying smile, the one he only used when he was on stage or flirting with someone. "Nice to meet you, Tiffany. Thanks for coming to the show."

I turned away—I didn't need to see or hear the next part— but I still caught Tiffany saying, "I love your band *so* much. Here, I got you a beer."

So that's why she had two drinks. I'd never stood a chance. Rejection always sucked, but being passed up for your older, better-looking, more talented brother every single time?

Yeah, that got old real fast.

Hector joined me as I made my way back to the bar. He was perpetually single, too, so at least we could stick together and roll our eyes at Jared and his harem of groupies.

"He's starting early, I see," Hector said.

"He probably figures he can hook up with this one now and then find a second girl for later." I kicked at a plastic cup on the floor. Bitter? Me? No, definitely not.

"That must be it." We ordered two beers, and then Hector turned to me. "Where's Becca?"

"She was supposed to meet us here at 6:30." I checked the time on my phone. 7:00 PM. "She must be running late. I'll text her."

"She better not bail on us," Hector said, removing his Villain Complex baseball cap and then shoving it back over his dark mop of curly hair. He always did that when he was stressed or pissed about something. Hector had been Jared's best friend since high school, and he'd become almost like a second brother to me over the years. It was usually my job to calm him down when he got like this.

"She wouldn't do that," I said. "Don't worry. She'll be here."

"I don't know, man. She's been acting weird."

Now that he mentioned it, Becca had been late to practice all week, and she'd seemed especially moody, too. But Becca was often like that. She'd never taken our practices as seriously as the rest of us did, so I figured she'd been having an especially bad week.

Becca was the latest in a long string of short-term bassists. She'd joined the band a couple months ago after Jared met her at a party. We'd lost our previous bassist when Jared had kicked him out of the band for stealing money from us to buy meth. So far we hadn't had too many problems with Becca, and I'd hoped that our bad luck was over.

I sent her a text asking if she was almost here and took a sip of my beer. "I'm sure she's on her way. There's plenty of time before our set."

The first USC band started playing, but the singer shrieked like a parrot being strangled and the rest of the band sounded like they'd learned how to play their instruments a week ago. The feedback blasting through the speakers was the best part of the song.

"My ears are bleeding," I yelled at Hector over the noise. "Make it stop."

"It's not that bad," Hector said, but he cringed when the drummer dropped one of his sticks and had to stop playing to pick it up. "Nope, I take that back."

"I don't know if I'll be able to get through all fifteen minutes of their set without my head exploding."

"Let's pray the other USC bands are as bad as they are." He gestured across the room with his beer. "I'm going to say hi to the guys from Twisted Regime. I'll catch up with you later."

He took off toward one of the UCLA bands we often played with, and I decided I'd had enough of this torture. I walked past Jared, who was still leaning against the wall, now with Tiffany pressed against him. He held the drink she'd given him in one hand and trailed the other up and down her back. She tilted her head up and said something that made him grin, and then he kissed her right there in front of me.

Ugh. My brother always worked fast, but it'd be nice if I didn't have to see it all the damn time. The worst part was there were other girls hovering nearby, hoping for their chance with him soon. Hello, I was right there and available. But no one looked at me as I brushed past them and through the door.

It wasn't much quieter backstage, and worse, it reeked of piss, weed, and cheap cologne. The area was tiny—little more than a hallway, really—and filled to the brim with the other bands standing around waiting for their sets. Graffiti had been scrawled across every inch of the walls underneath faded and ripped posters of bands like Bad Religion and the Sex Pistols. Dim lighting barely concealed the empty plastic cups, used ticket stubs, and god only knew what else that littered the floor.

I slipped off to a corner to sip my beer in peace and check out our competition. Tonight four bands from each college would compete against each other to win a $1,000 prize and a gig next month at a bigger club on Hollywood Boulevard, along with a $1,000 donation to the winning college's music program. USC had won the last two years, so the pressure was on for us to end their streak. Not to mention, we really wanted that gig. This was our chance to finally break out, to move beyond playing frat house parties and underground shows in the UCLA parking lot.

One band stood out from the others in pastel-colored shirts, khaki shorts, and shoes that looked more suited to taking daddy's boat for a spin than going to a club like this. With their frat boy looks and entitled smiles, I could almost guarantee they were from USC, and in the middle of them was Todd, another one of our former bassists.

Had Todd joined a new band? He went to USC so it was possible, but I couldn't imagine anyone actually putting up with the guy. Maybe he'd only recently joined and his bandmates hadn't yet realized what a dick he was. They'd find out soon enough like we had.

A girl showed up and started talking to Todd with one hand on her hip, her long, bright-red hair trailing down her back. Not natural red, but Starburst red. Hot Tamale red. Like candy I'd like to take a bite of. She had her back to me but wore a black leather jacket and jeans tight enough to show off her perfect ass. She tucked her hair behind her ear, and I caught a glimpse of a tattoo on her wrist. Hot. Too bad she was with Todd.

She raised a professional-looking camera and peered through it, taking shots of Todd's band. Maybe she wasn't actually with him, but a photographer for the show. My theory seemed to be confirmed when she turned to snap a few photos of the chaos around us.

I kept my eyes on her as she moved through the crowd, trying to get a glimpse of her face. But when she lowered her camera, the entire world stopped.

I recognized her.

I hadn't seen her in years and she looked completely different now, but I'd know that face anywhere. Those bright green eyes, those lush red lips, that smooth pale skin with the hint of freckles across her tiny nose. The girl I would never forget, the girl I could never get over.

Alexis Monroe.

CHAPTER TWO

What was Alexis doing here? She was supposed to be at Princeton, not here in LA and definitely not at our show tonight. Maybe she was with Todd's band. He was exactly her kind of guy, living off daddy's money and taking the private jet on vacations. But still, it was Todd. I thought she had better taste than that.

For a split-second, I debated whether I could duck out or hide or something, but she paused with her camera half-raised to her face, her eyes wide and her lips parted. She'd seen me. It was too late to escape.

We stared at each other for the longest minute of my life. She looked so different it was hard to believe it was actually her. Gone was her preppy image, with the stuffy cardigans and sensible shoes. In her leather jacket and studded boots, she looked like she belonged with our band, not Todd's. And her hair…it had always been red, but when we were in high school, it had been natural red. A soft ginger color. Copper and bronze. The color of the sun as it set over the horizon. I'd spent hours running my fingers through it and watching the strands glow as the light hit them. Now it was Maraschino cherry red, but still just as beautiful.

And that was definitely a tattoo on her wrist, though I couldn't tell what it was from this distance. She'd told me she would never get another tattoo, not after the ones we'd gotten together. What had changed in the past three years?

Of course, I looked different, too. My hair was dyed black now and longer, with an annoying tendency to fall in my eyes instead of sticking up like Jared's did. I'd added round black gauges to my ears, and I had more tattoos—not just on my arms, but across my chest, up my neck, and down my fingers. We'd both changed. My change just hadn't been quite as dramatic as hers because I'd already been halfway there when we'd broken up. Hell, that was one of the reasons she'd dumped me: that we were too different from each other and I wouldn't fit in with her new Princeton lifestyle. Kind of ironic that she had now fallen to the dark side herself.

Everything else faded away until it was only Alexis and me and all of our history stretching between us. Memories flashed through my mind like a slideshow. The first time we'd talked in tenth grade English class, when I'd finally worked up the courage to say hello to the girl so completely out of my league. The first time we'd kissed, in front of my piano after I'd tried—and failed—to teach her to play it. The first time we'd had sex, in her room surrounded by pink walls while her parents were out of town. Sneaking out to concerts using fake IDs. Practicing with the band while she watched and did her homework. Studying for the SATs together. Prom night. And finally, graduation—the last time I'd seen her.

What was I supposed to do? Walk over and say, *Hey, how's it going? How have you been since you ripped out my heart, tore it into a thousand pieces, and stomped all over it?* I could ignore her and walk away before things got weird, try to avoid her for the rest of the night. No, hiding would seem weak, like I wasn't over her or something. That was out, which meant I had to man up and talk to her.

I pushed off the wall and made my way through the throng of people, and she ditched Todd's band to meet me halfway. She stood a little straighter as I neared but was still a few inches shorter than me. The perfect height for our bodies to fit together. I moved to hug her, either out of habit or because it seemed the natural thing to do, but I shoved my hands in my pockets instead.

"Alexis," I said. "Long time, no see."

"Kyle," she said, in that breathy voice I knew too well, the one she used when she was excited. I'd heard her say my name like that many times—along with, *Oh god* and *Don't stop* and *Yes!*

I quickly pushed those memories aside. Thinking about Alexis like that would get me both turned on and depressed, and that combo couldn't lead to anything good. Especially since her body was as amazing as I remembered, with large, round breasts and curvy hips I wanted to run my hands over. I tried not to stare, but she gave me a dazzling smile that reeled me back in.

"It's so good to see you," she said, and I could tell from the way her face lit up that she meant it.

"What are you doing in LA? I thought you were at Princeton."

"I was for the first two years, but I transferred to USC for my junior year."

She'd been back in LA for months and hadn't contacted me all this time? I wasn't surprised exactly. She'd made it clear that we were done and she wanted nothing to do with me. But it still hurt a little.

I started to ask her why she'd come back to LA, but then it would seem like I cared and I didn't want that. "You look different. Your hair...I like it."

"Oh, thanks," she said, smoothing a loose curl. "My parents hate it."

"I bet."

"You look different, too. The hair, your tattoos…" Her lips quirked up, and her gaze traveled below my waist and then back to my face. "You look really good."

There went my plan of not getting turned on. I coughed and adjusted my weight, trying to hide the growing bulge in my jeans. "What are you doing here tonight?"

"I'm taking photos for the school paper." She gestured behind her at Todd and his friends, who were chugging drinks and pumping their fists like they were at a football game.

"You know those guys?" I asked, hoping she'd say no.

"Yep, they're one of the USC bands. Rubber Horse."

I cringed. Their name was an obvious play not just on the USC mascot, but also the condom brand and the Trojan horse from myth. Exactly the kind of thing Todd would choose.

"I didn't know you were going to be here," Alexis blurted out. "I didn't see Cross Paths listed on the lineup."

Wow, I'd forgotten how bad our original band name had been, back when Jared and I were dumb kids who thought using our last name was a good idea. "We're called Villain Complex now."

Her head tilted as she considered it. "Villain Complex…. I like it."

"Jared came up with it."

"Why am I not surprised?" She laughed. "How's he doing? Is he here? And Hector?"

"They're both by the bar. They're…good." I tried to think of what else I could say about them. When you haven't seen someone in years, it's hard to know how much info to give about everything they'd missed. "Jared graduated last year, and now he manages the band and works as a bartender. Hector finished art school and has a graphic novel coming out later this month."

"That's great. I'd love to see them again."

"Um, that might not be such a good idea."

"Oh…" Her face fell, her smile vanishing. "They probably hate me, huh?"

"They're…not your biggest fans, no."

"I guess I understand that." She took a step closer, looking up at me with hopeful eyes. "What about you? Do you hate me, Kyle?"

She smelled faintly of strawberries, and I had to look away before I did something stupid—like kiss her or push her away, I wasn't sure which. Did I hate her? Maybe once, but the anger was long gone now. After I'd started college, I'd moved on and tried to forget her. I thought I'd succeeded, too, until tonight. Now all the old scabs had fallen off and started bleeding again.

"No, I don't hate you."

She exhaled in a rush. "Good. Because I was hoping we could get a drink and catch up."

A part of me jumped to say yes, but I forced it down. I needed this conversation to end so I could escape and then avoid her for the rest of the night. The longer I was in her presence, the more I ached to touch her, the more I remembered how good she'd felt in my arms, the more I wanted to kiss her again. The nostalgia for what we'd once had was so strong it was almost crippling.

"Look, Alexis, I..." I trailed off, trying to find the right words. "It's just not a good idea. I'm sorry. But it was good to see you again. Really."

A flash of pain crossed her face. "Oh. Okay. Yeah. Maybe some other time."

The look in her eyes as I walked away made me feel like a total ass, but what else could I do? Spending even these few minutes with her had been torture. There were too many memories between us, both good and bad, and I didn't need to relive them again. Three years ago, I'd have done anything to make it work with her, even long distance, but she'd said no. I'd wanted forever, but she'd told me it was over, that she didn't love me anymore, that she was too good for someone like me.

And no matter how different she seemed or how hurt she looked, when she rejoined Todd and his friends I knew nothing had changed.

CHAPTER THREE

I finished my beer outside in the parking lot behind the club. It was quiet there or as quiet as it could be with the sounds of traffic and palm trees crashing in the wind. The Santa Anas were kicking up again tonight, drying out my eyes with warm gusts that blew trash everywhere. Still, it was better than being inside where my options were to listen to that band butcher their instruments, watch Jared make out with someone, or talk to my ex-girlfriend. I couldn't stay outside all night, but this seemed the safest way to avoid Alexis for as long as possible.

I kept picturing her face when I'd turned her down, how

vulnerable and hurt she'd looked. Maybe I'd made a mistake saying no so fast. Her sudden appearance had completely thrown me off and scrambled my brain, and even now I could barely accept that she was really here. I just needed some time to process that she was back in my life. Once the shock of it wore off, I could figure out what to do about her.

Besides, I had bigger things to worry about. It was 7:25 PM, and Becca hadn't texted me back or arrived yet. I tried calling her, but it went straight to voicemail. I hung up without leaving a message. Where the hell was she? We still had three hours before our set, but I was starting to get a bad feeling. I texted her again, just in case.

The back door banged open, and Todd came through, followed by his other band members. I turned in the opposite direction and played on my phone, hoping they wouldn't bother me.

"I thought I saw you in there, emo boy," Todd said with that shit-eating grin that never left his face. "Don't tell me your band actually got into this thing?"

I took a deep breath, trying not to let him get to me. "Top spot for UCLA, actually. You?"

"Same, for USC."

Each band had been ranked by the Battle of the Band organizers based on talent and popularity, with the top band from each school playing at the end of the night when there would be more people to vote for the winner. Todd's band must be pretty good to get the highest ranking for USC. Then again, based on that other band I'd just heard, maybe not.

"Where's Jared?" Todd asked. "I know you never go anywhere without your big brother's permission."

"Hilarious." I gestured at his entourage. "How'd you convince these guys to play with you? Did you have to pay them?"

"I got my own band together after I left yours. Turns out I was better off without you losers holding me back." He laughed, and his cronies behind him joined in with identical chortles. I wanted to punch each of them in the face to wipe off those arrogant smirks.

"After you *left*? More like after we kicked you out."

We'd tried to work with Todd—we really had. He was a good bassist, but after a few weeks, we'd all had it with his entitled attitude and dickish behavior so Jared got rid of him before things escalated. Good thing, too, because I doubted Hector could have refrained from bashing his head in much longer. Really, Todd should be thanking us.

"Do you even have a bassist now?" Todd asked. "I heard you've gone through a bunch since me. Guess I'm a tough act to follow, huh?"

"We have one. She's better than you, actually."

"A chick? Let me guess, Jared's screwing her on the side, too?" He made exaggerated humping motions, and all the other guys joined in, adding sounds to go with their movements. In case anyone around us had missed what huge douchebags they were. I felt dirty just standing near them.

"Real classy," I said. "And no. He's a professional. But you wouldn't know anything about that, obviously."

Hector walked out before Todd could piss me off any further. He quickly sized up what was going on and moved to my side, crossing his arms. "Hello, Todd."

He smirked. "Hey, *amigo*. Good to see they haven't shipped you back to Mexico yet."

Every muscle in Hector's body tensed. "What the fuck did you just say to me?"

Wow, I'd thought I couldn't hate Todd any more, but he'd just proven me wrong. It wasn't the first comment he'd made like that—once he'd asked Hector if he had swam here from Mexico—but it shocked me every time. This one was especially bad, though, because Hector's parents had been deported when he was a kid, leaving him with his grandmother and his three little sisters. I doubted Todd knew that, but that didn't excuse him being a racist shit.

He was an idiot if he wanted to mess with Hector, even with his three friends at his back. Hector worked out a ton to keep up his stamina for shows, and he'd been in plenty of fights before. He could probably take all four of these guys and not even break a sweat.

"Just messing with you, bro." Todd did that arrogant laugh again. This time his friends didn't join in.

Hector's hands clenched into fists, and a vein in his neck

throbbed. I was tempted to let him knock Todd out—hell, I was pretty close to joining in myself—but we couldn't afford to get in a fight and risk getting kicked out of the competition.

I put a hand on Hector's shoulder. "Let's go inside."

"Yeah, run back to big brother!" Todd called as we headed for the door. Hector stiffened and I thought he would turn back, but he shook it off and we made it inside without throwing any punches.

"I hate that guy," Hector muttered.

"Who doesn't? Todd wins Asshole of the Year every year. Don't let him get to you."

We returned to the main room where our friends, Twisted Regime, were on stage doing an AFI cover. I didn't see Alexis anywhere. Not that I was looking for her.

Okay, I was totally looking for her. But only so I could avoid her. That was it. Really.

I checked my phone again. Still nothing from Becca. I sent her yet another text, this time with a lot of exclamation points, but I didn't think that would get answered, either.

Jared joined us, and I was relieved to see he was alone. "Is Becca here?"

"I tried calling and texting, but she won't answer," I said.

"Shit." Jared ran a hand through his spiked-up hair, stress starting to peek through on his face. He was good at keeping it hidden, but I knew what to look for. "She knows how important this show is. She's coming, right?"

"She's probably running late." I didn't believe that, but I didn't want Jared to freak out. I quickly changed the subject. "Todd's here, though, with a new band. They've got the top spot for USC."

Jared's eyebrows shot up. "Who did he blow to get that?"

"Who knows? Probably paid someone off. Hector nearly took his head off outside."

"I'm sure he deserved it."

"Damn straight," Hector said.

"Oh, he did," I said. "He made another racist comment to Hector and said you were screwing Becca. What a jackass."

Jared coughed. "He said that?"

"Yeah." I rolled my eyes, but something about Jared's expression made me pause. He looked almost...guilty. "Oh, hell no. Don't tell me he's right?"

"I'm not *screwing* her..." He trailed off and rubbed the back of his neck.

I finished the sentence for him as it all came together in my head. "But you did."

It wasn't a question, and yet I hoped he would deny it. Every part of me wanted to believe my brother wouldn't be stupid enough to hook up with Becca, not when we'd finally found a good bassist, scored a decent gig, and had a shot at winning an even better one. But he looked away, and I knew the answer.

That's it. I was going to kill my brother.

"What the fuck, Jared?" Hector asked, echoing my thoughts exactly.

He held up his hands in surrender. "It was last week, after the parking lot show. We were drunk, she started taking her clothes off, one thing led to another…. I didn't mean for it to happen, I swear."

"That doesn't make it okay!" I couldn't believe he'd do this. Yes, Jared got around, and yes, it had been obvious to everyone that Becca wanted him. But the band *always* came first to Jared, and he must have known this would only mess things up.

"It was a stupid mistake, and we both agreed it was just a dumb hook-up and didn't mean anything. I thought she was fine with it. But at that party last night, she caught me making out with another girl and nearly took my head off, so I guess she's not as fine with it as she said."

"You think?" I snapped. No wonder Becca hadn't shown up.

"I'm sorry, okay? I didn't think it would be a problem."

Hector glared at him. "No because you never think with anything other than your dick."

Jared frowned but didn't answer. Probably because he knew Hector was right. I rubbed my face, trying to wipe all of this away. How was I going to fix this?

"If Becca doesn't show up soon, we're fucked," Hector said.

Jared sighed. "I'd call her, but I doubt she'd listen to me."

"Let me handle it." I wanted to strangle my brother, but that wouldn't solve anything. He'd gotten us into this mess, and as usual, it was my job to get us out of it. I checked my phone. 7:40 PM. Only a few hours to find Becca before our set. I had to try. "Any idea where she is right now?"

"No clue. You could try her apartment, I guess."

"Where is it?"

He gave me the address, and I put it into my phone. Luckily she lived fairly close. As long as traffic wasn't too bad, I'd make it back with plenty of time to spare. Assuming she was at her apartment. If not, we were screwed.

"I'll go with you," Hector said.

"No, stay with Jared. If I run late, you two will have to set up all our gear. And if she does show up while I'm gone, you might need to stop them from killing each other."

Hector grunted. "Fine."

I held out my hand. "Keys."

Jared reluctantly dropped the keys in my palm. "Maybe I should go…" He didn't like anyone else driving the band's van, but tough shit.

"Hell no. You've done enough. Just stay here and try not to piss anyone else off." I gave Hector a look that I hoped conveyed, *Keep him out of trouble.* He nodded, so he must have gotten the gist.

I fumed the entire way to the van. How could Jared do this to us? How could Becca? I was pissed at my brother, but she was partly to blame, too. They both must have known what a bad idea sleeping together was at the time. I didn't care how drunk or horny they'd been; they should have thought about how this would affect the rest of us. But clearly they hadn't, and now I was cleaning up after my brother once again. Not exactly how I wanted to spend my Saturday night.

At least it got me out of having to avoid Alexis for the next hour or so.

I got in the van and put the key in the ignition, but when I turned it, nothing happened. What the…? I tried it again, and this time got a few pathetic noises from it but not much else. This must be a mistake. The van had worked fine when we'd arrived. I checked the dashboard but didn't see any warning lights, and we still had gas. It *should* work. I tried again. And again. Still nothing. Dammit!

I banged on the steering wheel, accidentally honking the horn. Could this night get *any* worse?

"Car trouble?" Alexis asked from outside my window.

And just like that, it did.

CHAPTER FOUR

I'd been so distracted trying to get the van to start I must not have noticed her approach. She leaned through the window to glance at the dashboard, giving me a glimpse down her shirt. "Need some help?"

I tilted my head back and closed my eyes, trying to block out the image of her impressive cleavage. That was the last thing I needed to deal with right now. Maybe if I waited a minute, everything would be fixed when I opened my eyes. The van would work, and Alexis would be gone. Or, even better, Becca would be standing there instead of Alexis. I held my breath and waited for a miracle.

"Where are you going, anyway?" she asked. "Aren't you on soon?"

She was still there. The eyes-closed plan was a total fail. Damn.

"Not until 10:30. Our bassist is missing and I need to track her down, but our fucking van won't start."

I tried it again, hoping the fifth time would be the charm, but it just made that pathetic sound. I considered popping the hood and checking the engine, but I'd have no clue what to look for. Cars weren't my thing, and Jared and Hector were just as useless with them as I was.

"I don't suppose you picked up anything about fixing cars at Princeton?" I asked.

"No. But I could drive you."

I'd been avoiding looking at her as much as possible, but now my gaze snapped to her face. "Don't you have work to do here?"

She shrugged and tossed back a lock of her fiery hair, revealing a view of her graceful neck. "I have all the photos I need for the moment. I'm just waiting around until Rubber Horse goes on stage. We should be back by then, right?"

"We better be. We're on right after them."

I tapped my fingers on the steering wheel and tried to think of some other option. I could call AAA, but it would take them too long to get here and they'd probably want to tow the van to a mechanic, anyway. Public transportation in LA was such a joke I'd never get to Becca's place and back in time. If there was anyone else I could ask for help, I would have, but Alexis was my only hope. Still, I hesitated. I wasn't sure I wanted to be alone in a car with her. I had a feeling if I did this I'd be starting down a path I wasn't sure I wanted to travel.

I wracked my brain for any other solution, but in the end, it was my only option. "Are you sure?" I asked, giving her one last chance to change her mind.

"I'm sure." She laid her red-tipped fingers on my arm, over my phoenix tattoo. "I want to help you."

I swallowed as heat rushed through me, like she'd ignited the inked flames she was touching, and hopped out of the van. "Okay. Thanks."

"My car's over here," she said, leading me to the other side of the parking lot.

"The same one as before?" We'd spent so much time in that old Mercedes back in high school. Truth be told, I was kind of excited to see it again.

"No, that one died a year ago. I have a MINI now."

"Too bad. We had some good memories in that car."

"We did." She gave me a sly smile. "Some *very* good memories in the backseat."

I coughed and tried to steer the conversation back to something less dangerous, but all I could think about was when we'd been together. "Remember that time we got lost on our way home from a concert in Pomona? And we ran out of gas in a shady part of LA and had to wait for Jared to come get us?"

"I remember. I was scared we were going to get carjacked, so you helped…distract me." She met my eyes. "You were so very good at distracting me."

Suddenly, all I could think about was how I'd like to distract her now. First, I'd tangle my fingers in that long, thick hair, getting a good hold of it. Then I'd tilt her head back so I could press my lips to her neck, to that spot just below her ear. She'd moan my name, and I'd work my way down, lower and lower, dipping inside the V of her shirt to taste every inch of skin I'd seen earlier. She'd reach for the front of my jeans and—

Whoa there. None of those things could happen. I could not get involved with Alexis again, and the only way I'd get through the night was to banish those thoughts entirely. Why was she even bringing all of that up again? Earlier she'd mentioned wanting to catch up, and now she was flat-out hitting on me. Did she want to get back together or something?

We stopped at a black MINI Cooper with white racing stripes across the hood. Not a car I'd ever picture her driving. Hmm, maybe she *had* changed.

"Nice car," I said. "Not much room in the backseat, though." Wait, why had I said that? It's like I couldn't stop myself from flirting with her, either.

"I bet we could still fit."

Her eyes swept over me again, and it took all my energy not

to press her back against the side of the car and devour her. I was so, so tempted to make a move, even though it was a terrible idea. Being around Alexis was causing my brain to not function properly. I wanted to blame my growing hard-on for rendering me stupid, but that wasn't the entire reason. All the memories of being with Alexis, combined with seeing her again, were turning me into a sentimental fool.

I cleared my throat and tore my gaze away. "Let's just find Becca, okay?"

"Sure," she said, but she sounded disappointed. Hell, I was, too. I wished I was more like Jared and could do random, meaningless hook-ups, but that wasn't me. If I got a taste of Alexis, I would only want more and more. I had to stop this now before it went any further.

Once in the car, I pulled up the directions on my phone, and we drove out of the parking lot in silence, save for the perky, robotic voice of the GPS. I tried to picture the most disgusting things I could to calm my raging sex drive. Dead cockroaches. Moldy sandwiches. Old people in hospital gowns.

"So…how have you been?" she asked.

Did she actually care or was she making small talk to pass the time? When someone asked a question like that, they never wanted a real response. They just wanted to hear that you were fine. I didn't know what to tell her.

She glanced at my face and laughed.

"What?" I asked.

"I know that look."

"What look?"

"That one where you're trying to figure me out. It's just a simple question, Kyle."

Simple. Sure. Let's see, last time we'd spoken she'd broken up with me and moved across the country, taking my heart with her and turning me into a puzzle with pieces missing. Since then, I'd gone to UCLA, dated a couple girls I could barely remember, and drowned myself in the band with Jared and Hector. And somewhere along the way, I'd tried to find another girl to replace Alexis and failed over and over again.

But I just said, "I've been good. You?"

"Me too. I guess. Princeton wasn't really my scene. Too stuffy and uptight. Too much like my parents."

"Sounds familiar..."

"Yeah, yeah, you told me so and all that. I knew it would be like that, but I didn't realize just how much I would hate it. Or how much I would miss LA." She glanced at me, long and full of meaning, like I was a part of what she'd missed. "I'm still glad I went, though. It made me realize who I really was—and how much I wasn't like those people."

"That explains the new look."

She dressed now like she had when she'd sneaked out with me on dates. She'd leave her house in her floral dresses and pink heels, giving her parents some lie about going to a friend's house, and then would change into a tight black dress, fishnets, and combat boots in the car. I liked that she wasn't hiding that side of her anymore.

"I was tired of pretending to be someone I wasn't," she said. "As soon as I got back to LA, I tried to make the outer-me match the inner-me."

"It suits you. And the new ink, too."

She lifted up the sleeve of her leather jacket, revealing the tattoo I'd glimpsed before—a black aperture symbol on her wrist. "I got this once I decided on my major."

"What happened to psychology?"

She shrugged. "It wasn't for me. I can barely understand my own head half the time. Who am I to try to get inside someone else's? But one semester, I took a photography class and fell in love. I'm planning to go into photojournalism. What about you?"

"I'm a music major, mainly studying sound engineering and mixing."

"That's what you always said you wanted to do," she said, smiling. "And you got some new ink, too. I like them."

"Thanks." When we'd been together, I'd had a few already, but after I'd turned eighteen, I'd gotten full sleeves—a phoenix on one arm and a water dragon on the other, surrounded by flames, waves, and stars. Recently, I'd gotten the words *LIVE LOUD* across my knuckles, too.

"What's the story with the triangles?" she asked.

I had a triangle tattooed on each wrist, the left one all black and the right one hollow and inverted. "Jared and I got them not long after…" I was about to say, *not long after you left*, but that didn't seem very nice. "After I started college."

"You got matching tattoos?"

"Yeah. His are mirror images of mine. They symbolize brotherhood, duality, dark and light, inner and outer selves…" I shrugged. "That sort of thing."

It sounded stupid when I said it all out loud, but they were my favorite tattoos. Once, Jared had been the golden boy, the one who could do no wrong, who'd gotten everything he wanted and made our parents proud. Growing up, I'd been the one who'd gotten tattoos and sneaked out to goth clubs, who'd been caught stealing booze from a liquor store and barely gotten away with a warning, who'd nearly been kicked out of school for smoking pot. And Jared had been there to rescue me time and time again. But over the last few years, we'd switched places. Or maybe we were both stumbling through the dark together, looking for the light to find our way again.

"I like them," Alexis said. "Do you still have our tattoo?"

"Of course."

"Me too." We stopped at a red light, and she lifted the hem of her shirt, revealing the infinity symbol peeking out above her jeans. Damn, she was sexy, showing off that tiny glimpse of bare skin. Was she *trying* to make me crazy?

Two could play at that game. I raised the bottom of my shirt, flashing the matching tattoo on my hip. It must have worked because she reached across to brush the ink with her cool fingers.

I held still as she traced the symbol slowly, like she couldn't stop herself. Even the slightest touch from her awakened parts of me I'd thought long dead. I was frozen in place, wishing she would smooth that hand up across my chest. Or even better, dip those fingers inside the waist of my jeans and move lower…

The light changed, and she yanked her hand away. "Sorry."

"It's fine." It was so not fine.

"No, I shouldn't have done that. I just couldn't resist."

"Don't worry about it." I adjusted in the seat, trying to get comfortable again. It was unfair how easily she excited me. All she'd done was touch me, and I'd instantly turned into a horny, single-minded male. Pathetic. I wasn't sixteen anymore. I needed to get control of myself before I did something I'd regret.

I stared out the window, willing my body to relax. I'd known this car ride would be a bad idea. We hadn't arrived at Becca's place yet, and I was already losing my damn mind. Not because of the lust—though that was definitely a problem—but because of all the memories that kept coming back to me. Like when we'd gotten the tattoos and how we'd held hands the entire time, helping each other be strong through the pain, believing we would be together forever. The infinity symbol had been a promise to each other, the kind only stupid kids in love for the first time would make. I'd thought about covering it up many times, but I'd never been able to go through with it. Maybe a part of me was still hoping for forever.

And Alexis still had the tattoo, too.

CHAPTER FIVE

It took us a good ten minutes of circling the area before we found a parking space we could squeeze into near Becca's place. The wind had gotten worse, and palm fronds were scattered across the sidewalk, forming an obstacle course on the way to her apartment building. We headed up stairs with peeling paint and a broken handrail. I checked the address on my phone again and rang the doorbell.

No one answered. What would we do if she wasn't home? I had no backup plan. Going to her place was all I'd come up with. I rang the doorbell again. And again.

A girl with a nose ring finally opened the door, and with her came the strong smell of clove cigarettes. "Yeah?"

"Hey, I'm Kyle. I'm in a band with Becca. Is she here?" I tried to peek into the dark room behind her, but I didn't see Becca's blue hair anywhere.

"Nope," the girl said, sounding bored.

"Do you know where she is?"

"Nope."

Wow, could she be any less helpful? "Could you text her or something? Do you have *any* idea where she could be?"

The girl huffed. "How should I know? I'm not her babysitter."

She started to close the door, but Alexis slammed her palm against it, holding it open. "We need to find Becca *now*, and we're not leaving until you tell us where she is."

The girl chewed on her lip while Alexis stared her down. She shrugged. "Becca won't answer my texts, but she's probably at the bar on the corner. That's where she likes to hang out when she's in one of these moods."

"See, that wasn't so hard, was it?" Alexis asked. She released the door and stepped back, flashing me a triumphant grin. She'd never looked sexier.

"If you find Becca, tell her she owes me money for rent." The girl mumbled something else under her breath and then shut the door in our faces.

"Thanks for the help," I said to Alexis as we walked down

the stairs. She'd always been confident, but she had never been this bold before. I liked it. I just prayed Becca was actually at this bar, or we'd be in big trouble.

"You were being too nice," she said.

"Yes, that is a problem I have."

She took my arm, turning me around. She stood a step above me, putting us at the same height. "Maybe it's time to be not so nice for a change."

"Oh, yeah?" I moved close enough to feel her breath on my cheek. I knew I was flirting with her again, but I couldn't help myself. "And what would a not-so-nice guy do right now?"

"Hmm…try to kiss me?" she suggested, with that breathless, excited voice I knew so well.

Her parted lips were an invitation, and I trailed a finger down her cheek, unable to stop myself. It would be so easy to lean in and press my mouth to hers, to slide my arms around her waist and pull her against me, to feel her body along mine. Every inch of me strained to close the distance between us.

I didn't know if I could let her into my heart a second time, but that didn't stop me from wanting her. If anything, I wanted her more because of the danger. Alexis was an open flame, and I was drawn to her deadly beauty. I wanted her to burn me all over again.

I traced my thumb along her bottom lip, but when her eyes fluttered shut, I dropped my hand and turned away. "Good thing I'm a nice guy then."

She sighed but didn't say another word as we walked down the block in search of the bar.

I had to stay focused. My goals were to get Becca, return to the club, and win the Battle. I repeated those three things in my head like a mantra, trying to distract myself from Alexis's far-too-tempting body beside me.

I spotted Becca as soon as we turned the corner. She was leaning against the outside of the bar, smoking a cigarette like she had all the time in the world, like we weren't all waiting for her or spending our entire night tracking her down.

"Hey, Kyle." She took a long drag. "I heard you used to be able to smoke inside bars in LA. Wouldn't that be nice?"

"Where the hell have you been?"

She shrugged. "Here and there."

I wanted to yell at her, to shake her and ask her why she'd abandoned us tonight, but something in her face stopped me. I had a feeling yelling at her wouldn't help. "How are you doing?"

"How am I *doing*?" She snorted. "I'm great. Don't I *look* great?"

Not in the slightest. Her short, blue hair stuck out all over the place, her eyes were bloodshot and dripped black like a goth clown, and her tank top and jeans were ripped and barely hanging together with a few choice safety pins. On second thought, her clothes always looked like that.

But the thing that alarmed me most was that her words were slurred like she was drunk. I had never seen her flat-out drunk before, and I wasn't sure if she could play like that. I wasn't willing to risk it, not with a gig this important. I'd have to get her sobered up fast, assuming I could even convince her to come with us.

I took a minute to consider my words while she blew smoke in my direction. "Becca, I get why you're upset. Jared told me what happened, and the way he treated you sucks. It really does. But we can't go on stage without you. If you don't come to the show tonight, we're *all* screwed."

She flicked ashes toward the street. "I know. Don't care."

"I don't believe that."

After all the hours practicing together, she had to care a *little*. She'd been a part of Villain Complex for a few months, and I'd thought we were becoming something close to friends in that time. But even if she didn't care, I was desperate. If I had to resort to begging on my knees in the middle of the street, so be it.

"Look, whatever this thing is with Jared, we'll work it out. I promise. Just come with us to the club. Please, Becca."

"There's nothing to work out. Your brother's a dick. I'm done with the band. End of story."

I tugged on the gauges in my ears, trying to hold on to my last remaining slivers of calm. I couldn't be too mad at her when part of this was Jared's fault, but she'd known what my brother was like and had still gotten involved with him. They were both to blame for this mess, and I was stuck in the middle. Leave it to

Kyle to fix everyone's problems—again. But I got the feeling, no matter what I said, Becca would never come to the show. She didn't care that she was screwing over me and Hector; she was too mad at my brother to see beyond anything else. And time was ticking away while we argued about it.

"Jared *is* a dick," Alexis said. I scowled at her—yes, he was a dick sometimes, but he was my brother, too—but she ignored me and continued. "But Kyle's *not*. He came all the way out here to make sure you were okay. He's a good guy, and he doesn't deserve this. Quit the band tomorrow if you have to, but do this one show tonight...for him."

"Who the hell are you?" Becca asked.

"Alexis." Her eyes flicked to me for a second. "I'm Kyle's...friend."

I fully expected Becca to tell Alexis to piss off, but she just stared at the passing cars while she smoked. Finally, she said, "I thought things would be different, you know? After we hooked up."

I'd never heard her be so open before about anything, but maybe the alcohol was loosening her tongue. I placed a hand on her shoulder. "I'm sorry, Becca. But you know how Jared is. He doesn't do relationships."

"I know. I *know*." She slumped against the wall, eyes closed. "I only joined your stupid band to get close to him, and now I can't even look at him. Or you, Kyle." She took another long drag off her cigarette. "God, I wish he was more like you."

I wanted to say, *If Jared was more like me, you wouldn't have slept with him.* But I think we both knew that, even without saying it. "Becca, it doesn't matter why you joined the band. You're a damn good bassist, and we don't want you to leave. Please do this show with us tonight."

I was about to give up and resort to full-out begging, but she put her cigarette out on the wall behind her and pushed off with a kick of her combat boots. "Fine. Let's go."

"Thank god." My shoulders sagged with relief. "I mean, thanks."

"Yeah, well, I was planning on coming to the show eventually," Becca said. "I just wanted Jared to sweat a little first."

I wasn't sure I believed that, but my good-guy status was working in my favor for once, so I wasn't going to argue. As long as we got through the Battle, I'd deal with everything else later. Even if it meant finding yet another bassist.

CHAPTER SIX

We stopped at Becca's place to pick up her gear (while her roommate yelled about the rent again), and then she squeezed into the backseat of Alexis's car. I was starting to think we'd actually make it back to the club in time—or even be early—until Becca burped behind us, making the car reek of alcohol.

"We need to get her sobered up fast," I said to Alexis.

"I'm *fine*," Becca said. "I just had a couple beers. And some tequila. Not a problem. I can totally play like this."

"She needs some carbs and coffee, stat," Alexis said. "How about that Denny's on Sunset Boulevard? The one we used to go to after concerts?"

I couldn't help but smile at the memory of all those late nights, but I shook my head. "That would take too long. Let's just hit a drive-thru."

"One drive-thru coming up."

She returned my smile, and all the reasons why I couldn't get involved with her again started to dissolve. I placed my hand on hers when she went to shift gears, to silently thank her for all her help. Without her, I'd still be stuck in that parking lot yelling at our stupid van.

"So what's the deal with you two?" Becca asked, ruining the moment. "Are you dating?"

"No," I said, jerking my hand back.

"We did, once," Alexis said, as she pulled away from the curb.

Becca leaned between us, and the whiff of beer and cigarettes made me almost gag. "Ooh, are you getting back together?"

"No!" I didn't want to discuss my love life with a drunken Becca, of all people. "Alexis just happened to be at the show tonight taking photos for USC."

"Actually…that's not *entirely* true," Alexis said.

My head snapped back to her. "What?"

She gave me a hesitant look before focusing on the road again. "Promise you won't get mad?"

"No, that question pretty much guarantees that whatever you say is going to upset me."

"Okay, here goes." She sucked in a breath, like she was

steeling herself for what might come next. "Earlier I said I didn't know you'd renamed the band, but that wasn't true. I've been following you guys this entire time. I thought, if I came back to LA, we might be able to start over again, and when I saw you were doing this show, I had to come. Taking photos for the school paper was just an excuse I made up." She blurted out the words, like she had to get them out before she lost her nerve. "I know it sounds crazy, but I had to try at least. I had to see you."

"But...why?" I wasn't sure if I was asking why she'd lied or why she'd been following the band or why she'd had to see me. Option D: all of the above.

She bit her lip, giving me another quick glance. "I...I missed you."

"You *missed* me?" My voice grew louder, filling up the small car, but I couldn't help it. "You were the one who broke up with me!"

"I know. And I'm sorry." She gripped the steering wheel harder. "God, I'm an idiot. I don't know why I thought you'd be happy to see me."

"So Kyle was the one who got dumped," Becca interrupted. "Very interesting."

"Shut up, Becca!" I stared at Alexis, studying her face. She seemed sincere, but did she really think she could show up tonight and apologize and I'd be cool with everything? That we could pick up where we'd left off? She said she missed me, but why would anything be different this time? "Look, Alexis.

Things have changed a lot since high school and—"

"You know, this all makes sense now," Becca continued, leaning over my shoulder. "Kyle hasn't had a girlfriend the entire time I've known him. Can you believe that? He's a good-looking guy, so I thought maybe he was gay or something, but then I caught him checking out my boobs so I knew *that* wasn't the case. Or, at least, I figured he swung both ways. But I guess he just wasn't over you."

"He does like boobs," Alexis agreed.

Becca snorted. "Don't all guys?"

"That is *not* true," I got out through gritted teeth. I didn't want Alexis to think I'd been pining over her all this time. Yes, I'd been going through a dry stretch lately, but that happened sometimes. Totally normal.

"What—that all guys like boobs?" Alexis asked.

"I guess some *are* probably ass men," Becca said with a drunk giggle. "Or, you know, into other guys."

I banged my head against the window, hoping it would knock me unconscious and get me out of this conversation. What would Jared do in this situation? Probably do his stupid wink and say something that convinced both girls to get into bed with him. Me? I was not that smooth.

"I've just been busy with school and the band," I muttered. Becca giggled again, and I seriously considered opening the car door and throwing myself into the street. "I've had other girlfriends, okay?"

"Of course," Alexis said, but she fidgeted in her seat and frowned. "So you've dated a lot of girls since me?"

Talk about a loaded question. There was no safe answer to that. "Why do you care?"

"I don't. I just…" She shook her head. "Never mind."

"No, really, what kind of question is that?" I asked, getting even more riled up. "If I say no, will that make you happy? Or do you want me to say yes so you won't feel guilty? Do you *really* want to hear about the other girls I've been with?"

"Oh, this is getting good," Becca said, wedging her head between us again.

"Shut up, Becca!" Alexis said.

She leaned back, raising her hands. "Hey, just pretend I'm not here. You two clearly have a lot of issues you need to work out."

"It was a stupid question," Alexis said to me. "Forget it."

This was so not the time to have this discussion, but I couldn't stop now. I'd held onto this shit for three years. It felt damn good to finally let it out. "At graduation, you told me you didn't love me anymore. That we were too different and I wouldn't fit into your new, perfect life at Princeton. You *broke* my heart, Alexis, so you're not allowed to be jealous of who I slept with after you left."

"I didn't *want* to leave you! You could have come to New Jersey with me! Even though you didn't get into Princeton, there were other colleges nearby—"

"But that was never my dream! My place was always here, with the band, with my brother. I couldn't leave them behind."

"So I should have given up *my* dream and stayed behind with you?"

"No, of course not! I never asked you to do that, but you didn't even want to go to Princeton. That was your father's dream, not yours!"

"That's not true! It had nothing to do with my dad—"

"It had *everything* to do with him and with your good-little-rich-girl image! You broke up with me because I wasn't part of his plan for you. I didn't fit into that lifestyle, with the country clubs and boat parties and fancy cars."

"That's not why I broke up with you!" She drew in a ragged breath. "Kyle, it never would have worked out between us."

"What's that supposed to mean?"

She sighed. "We would have tried to do the long-distance thing at first, but over time we would have talked less and less as we made other friends, experienced new things, chased different dreams. Eventually, our lives would've no longer overlapped and we wouldn't have anything to say to each other. I couldn't stand the idea of going through that, of us slowly growing to resent each other and our love fading away into nothing. That's why I lied and said I didn't love you—to save us from all of that heartache. I figured one quick moment of pain would be better than four drawn-out years of it. I thought I was doing the right thing for both of us."

"What about forever, Alexis?" I asked, touching the tattoo on my hip. "What's four years out of forever? I would have waited for you. I would have done *anything* to make you happy. But you gave up on us!"

"And I'm admitting that I made a mistake!"

"Damn, your make-up sex is going to be *awesome*," Becca said.

"Shut up, Becca!" we both yelled.

The car dropped into silence, with only the sound of the engine and the traffic around us to play a score for our thoughts. For years, I'd wondered what had changed between us at the end, why Alexis had stopped loving me. Or if she had ever loved me at all. I'd often dreamed of her running into my arms and telling me she'd made a mistake, but now that it had happened, I wasn't sure how I felt.

Yes, long distance would have been hard. Being thousands of miles apart for four years would have been torture, but I would have done it gladly. She'd *always* been the one, from the moment I'd seen her in English class. Like a fool, I'd meant it when I'd said forever, but I wasn't lying now when I said things had changed since high school. I wasn't the same stupid kid who believed in things like soul mates and love that lasted forever.

Even if I still loved her, I wasn't sure love was enough anymore.

CHAPTER SEVEN

We pulled into a Jack In The Box, and Becca groaned. "I don't feel good."

Alexis shot her a warning glance. "Don't you dare throw up in my car."

I scanned Becca's face, which had taken on a color only a few shades away from her hair. "We better go inside."

Alexis abandoned the drive-thru line and pulled into a parking spot. I hopped out and moved the seat up, but Becca didn't budge.

"C'mon, Becca," I said.

She moaned and then flopped to the side and practically rolled out of the car. I caught her arm to help her up, and she leaned against me while I led her inside. Everyone stared at us, either because of our kaleidoscope of hair colors or because Becca looked like she might hurl at any moment. How was she going to play tonight if she was like this?

"I'll get some food," Alexis said. "You stay with her." She got in line behind one of those guys with big, bushy beards that made you wonder whether he was homeless or just a hipster.

I dumped Becca into a booth and sat across from her. "Are you going to be sick?"

"I need a cigarette," she mumbled.

"Is that a no?"

She jumped up and ran into the bathroom, covering her mouth. I heard gagging sounds just as the door shut, so I guessed that answered my question.

Alexis was still at the counter, so I texted Jared to let him know the situation and then got up to knock on the bathroom door. "Becca, you okay in there?"

"Go away!" she yelled.

Well, at least she wasn't passed out on the floor. "Can I get you anything?"

"No!"

The sound of vomiting continued, and I raked my fingers through my hair. "All right. I'm out here if you need me."

I dropped back into the booth as Alexis returned with a tray of food. She slid in next to me, her arm brushing against mine. I tensed up but didn't move away, waiting to see if she would bring up our conversation from the car. I wasn't ready yet. The wound was still too raw and tender.

"How's she doing?" Alexis asked, and I relaxed.

"Not good."

"Maybe she'll feel better after she throws up."

"Maybe…" Or maybe we were completely screwed.

"I got her a breakfast meal. Pancakes, hash browns…. She'll be sober in no time." Alexis started arranging the food on the table. "Have you eaten anything?"

"No. Haven't had time."

"Here, I got you something." She slid a cheeseburger over to me, along with curly fries and a coffee. The cheeseburger even had bacon on it. All of my favorite things—she remembered.

"Thanks," I said as I took a bite. "Mmm…. Bacon makes everything better."

She unwrapped one of those tiny, crunchy tacos, and I burst into laughter. "What?" she asked.

"You're still eating those nasty things?"

She gave me a playful shove on the shoulder. "They are not nasty! Just because you once ate so many of them you got sick doesn't mean they're not delicious."

"Don't remind me," I said with a groan. "Damn, I can't believe you remember that."

"Of course I do. I remember everything, babe."

For a second, it was like we were in high school again on some crazy, late-night adventure. We'd always ended up in one food place or another, drunk on love and music and youth, and she'd always called me "babe."

We resumed eating, but my every sense was completely tuned to her body next to mine. I didn't taste any of my food; there was only her, living and breathing and real. No longer a ghost haunting my memories, but beside me again. Despite all the heartache, sitting so close to her felt natural, like the world had clicked back into alignment. Like I'd taken a big gulp of air after holding my breath too long.

I wanted to bring up our conversation from the car, but I wasn't sure how to ease back in without it turning into another fight. "Were your parents mad that you left Princeton?" There. That was relatively safe.

"They were disappointed, especially my dad, but they were happy I was back in California, too. Until they saw the tattoos and the hair, anyway. Then they wanted to disown me."

"Bet they would have loved to blame me for that one." Her parents had always hated me—for being in a rock band and having tattoos and generally being a "bad influence."

"I'm sure they wished they could have. What about your parents?"

I crumpled the empty burger wrapper in my fist. "I barely talk to them."

We'd been in high school when my parents had split up, and Jared and I had gotten stuck in the middle of their nasty divorce. Our parents fought over custody, over money, over the house, over everything down to a broken lamp in the garage. They each tried to get us to turn against the other parent, to give up information, to make us choose, but we wouldn't. Jared had taken it better than I had, of course. I'd been so angry, so willing to rage at anything and anyone, so eager to do anything to forget for a little while.

After I'd gotten caught stealing and almost gotten my dumb ass arrested, my parents had made me see a shrink. Then my dad had tried to get the shrink to testify that my actions showed that my mother was unfit to have custody over me. My mom had retaliated by bringing up my father's cocaine addiction and all his affairs. I'd spiraled lower and lower, hating them both, hating myself, wanting it all to end. One night, I'd tried to make the pain stop with pills and alcohol. That's when Jared had somehow convinced my parents to let him have custody of me until I turned eighteen. To this day, I still don't know how he did it, but I wouldn't be alive today without him. He'd helped me redirect my anger, and music became my savior.

And then I'd met Alexis and the world had truly seemed worth living in again. Like Jared, she'd believed in me, even when I was at my worst. With my history, I'd never expected to go to college, but she'd convinced me not to give up on school. She'd spent hours tutoring me to make sure my grades got better, making me take a hundred SAT practice tests until I got my scores up and helping me write entrance essays about how I'd turned my life around with the power of love and music and all that bullshit. It was only due to her tireless efforts that I'd gotten into UCLA at all.

"I'm sorry," Alexis said. "I know that's a sore subject."

I shrugged. If anyone knew what I'd been through with my parents, it was Alexis. "Their divorce went through finally. My mom moved to New York last year, but my dad's still in LA. I'm just glad they're not dragging us into court every week anymore."

"That's good." She pushed around a stray curly fry. "And Jared, he's…better?"

"Sort of. I mean, he's not drinking as much or getting into fights these days, at least. But he still has a new girl in his bed every other night."

At eighteen, Jared had given up his spot at Columbia and switched to UCLA at the last minute to take care of me. And yeah, he'd been a terrible cook, he'd sucked at keeping the house clean, and he'd shrunk all our laundry, but he'd also made sure the bills got paid, that I'd gotten to school every day, and that I'd had someone looking out for me, all while going to college himself. That was more than I could say for our parents.

So when Jared caught his long-term girlfriend sleeping with Ben—our first bassist and my best friend at the time—and snapped, I'd been there for him, too. For a year after that, it was a rare night when he hadn't stumbled home at 4 AM either drunk, with bloody knuckles and a black eye, or on the arm of some new girl. Or all of the above. He'd been a mess, and I couldn't have left him to go to college with Alexis. Jared had always been there when I'd needed him, so I'd done the same for him when he'd fallen apart. That's what brothers did: we stuck together, no matter what. Even if it meant giving up what we wanted.

Even if it meant losing the girl I loved.

"Same old Jared, then." A sad smile touched her lips. "I miss the Jared before all that, who'd help us with our homework and then make us popcorn and let us stay up all night watching horror movies."

"Me too. I think that Jared is gone for good, though. You saw what happened with him and Becca." I let out a bitter laugh. "You seem to be the one girl who can resist him."

She wrinkled her nose. "Oh, gross. He's like my big brother."

I couldn't help but smile. "Good."

"Trust me, you don't have anything to worry about there." She rested her hand lightly on mine, like she wasn't sure if I would pull away. "Kyle, it's *always* been you."

I missed this. The simple things, like holding her hand. The way she flipped her hair over her shoulder. The glint in her green eyes when she laughed at something I said. The freckles on her cute nose peeking out from under her makeup. The softness of her red lips, the delicate curve of her neck, the swell of her breasts…

I looked away, clearing my throat. "Alexis, what do you want from me?"

Her hand tightened around mine. "Three years ago, I made a huge mistake. It *killed* me to break up with you, and I've regretted it ever since. I should have tried to make it work long distance, but I messed up." Her voice trembled, but she went on. "I know you'll probably never forgive me for what I did, and I don't blame you. All I want now is a second chance to try to make it up to you. To do something different this time. To prove I never stopped loving you."

Her words woke up something within me—a memory of what we used to be and a spark of hope for what we might be again. "I *am* happy to see you," I admitted, referring to what she'd said in the car. "But why should I believe anything will be different this time?"

She raised her free hand to my cheek. "Because I've changed. I'm not afraid to be who I am anymore. I'm not afraid to fight for what I want. *Who* I want."

I wanted, more than anything, to believe her. I leaned into her touch, staring at the girl I had always loved, who said she still loved me. I didn't take my eyes off her as she trailed her fingers down, along my stubble, tracing my jaw. Her touch was soft but direct, like she was exploring the changes in my face since she'd last seen me. I held completely still. I didn't blink. I didn't breathe. If I moved, I'd break the spell over both of us.

Her fingers skimmed down my neck, and she laid her hand

against my chest, digging her fingers into my Joy Division T-shirt where it said, *Love Will Tear Us Apart*. She was already so close, her thigh pressed against mine in the tiny booth, her strawberry-and-spice scent tickling my nose with each breath. Being with her again was so familiar, so comfortable, so *right*. I couldn't stop myself from moving closer, resting my hand on the curve of her shoulder, lowering my head to hers. I closed my eyes, savoring that instant before our mouths met, before everything changed between us and there was no going back.

But I never got to kiss her because Becca slumped down in the booth across from us and groaned. I jerked away from Alexis, and the fog in my head cleared a little.

"You're back," I said, like an idiot.

Becca reeked of vomit and alcohol, but at least she'd returned to a normal color. She grabbed the coffee in front of her and started chugging it. "Were you two making out?"

"I wish," Alexis said with the hint of a smile.

Damn, we *had* been about to make out, right in the middle of a Jack In The Box with the hipster/homeless guy watching us from another booth. I needed to get a grip.

I reminded myself of my priorities: get Becca, return to the club, win the Battle. Becca. Club. Battle. Alexis was a distraction I didn't have time for at the moment, no matter how tempting she was.

"Are you feeling better?" I asked Becca. "'Cause we need to get going."

"Fine, let's go, but I'm taking this with me." Becca scooped up her breakfast meal as she stood up.

"Just don't get syrup all over my car," Alexis said.

"Deal."

She headed for the door, and for a moment, Alexis and I were alone in the booth again. Our eyes locked, and the electricity of our near-kiss crackled between us. If we touched, we'd surely set off sparks. I almost reached for her, anyway. It was so damn hard to leave her alone.

Focus, Kyle. Becca. Club. Battle. Later I'd figure out how I felt about Alexis and what I would do about it. Later I could kiss her for hours, if I wanted. But not now. I had to get my band back together first.

CHAPTER EIGHT

The LA traffic gods smiled on us for once. We got back to the club with a little over an hour to spare. Hector and Jared were already in the parking lot, watching while our van was hooked to a tow truck. Getting our gear home tonight was going to be a pain, but I added that problem to the list for later. I mentally crossed off *get Becca* and *return to the club*. Time to focus on item number three: win the Battle.

I let Becca out of the car, and she immediately lit up another cigarette. I stared over the hood at Alexis. We'd been quiet on the drive back, too conscious of Becca behind us, and in the silence, all my doubts had crept back in. Being around her was intoxicating, but when I stopped to think about getting involved with her again, my heart wanted to don battle armor to protect itself. I didn't trust her not to break me again.

I moved around the car to stand in front of her. "Thanks for helping me find Becca. I would have been screwed without you."

She smiled up at me with those dark red lips I'd so wanted to kiss. "It was my pleasure."

"About what we said..." I rubbed the back of my neck, unsure how to continue. I was tongue-tied and awkward, like I was sixteen all over again and asking Alexis out for the first time. "I need to think about it, okay?"

She bit her lip but nodded. "I understand."

I hated seeing her look so disappointed. "Maybe we can talk about this after the show. Or some other night. I just have a lot to deal with right now."

"Of course. The Battle. I can't wait to see you perform again. It's been a long time."

"Yeah." I glanced behind me in the direction of the other guys. "Um, I better go sort things out with the band before the show. I'll see you later, okay?"

Before I could think better of it, I wrapped my arms around her in a hug. She slid her hands up my back, pulling me closer, tucking her face into my neck. Her breasts flattened against my chest, and I buried my nose in her hair, savoring the feel of her against me, how perfectly we fit together, how amazing it was to hold her again. The wind kicked up around us, tearing at our hair and our clothes, and we pulled apart.

As she walked away, I admired the view from behind, resisting the urge to run after her. I shook it off and gestured for Becca to come with me. She groaned but tagged along, and we joined Jared and Hector on the other side of the parking lot as the van was being towed out of the lot.

"Hey," I said. "What's going on with the van?"

Jared ignored me and scanned Becca. "Where have you been?"

She waved her cigarette at him. "Don't even start."

His eyebrows shot up. "What's that supposed to mean?"

"Nothing," she snapped.

"No, what exactly is the problem? Is this about that night? 'Cause we both agreed that was a mistake. You said you were fine with it."

"I am fine with it! I'm just tired of your shit!"

I stepped between them, giving them each pointed looks. "Hey, as far as I'm concerned, you both messed up, but that's over now. It's done, it's in the past, and you both need to move on. We're a band, and we have to stick together if we want to win this thing. Can you two handle that?"

Jared's face went blank, putting his cool mask on again. "Of course."

Becca flicked ashes on the ground and said nothing. Hector took a sip of his beer and shook his head, like he was disappointed in all of us. So much for my rousing speech.

I sighed. "At least for tonight, let's try to keep it professional, okay?"

"Not a problem," Jared said, practically spitting the words out.

"Whatever." Becca dropped her cigarette and took off without another word, her heels clicking on the pavement.

"That went well," I muttered. If Jared and Becca got through the night without killing each other, it would be a miracle.

Behind us, someone sniggered. Todd leaned against a nearby parked car, looking like a cat who'd just caught a mouse. "Told you he was screwing her."

"What do you want, Todd?" I was too tired to deal with him on top of all the other shit going on.

"Oh, that's easy. I want to watch you lose. I want the three of you to walk off that stage with your tails between your legs, knowing I beat you."

"Keep dreaming," Jared said, crossing his arms. "We're going to crush you."

"Guess we'll see, won't we?" He flashed that cocky smirk and headed back to the club.

Hector downed the rest of his beer and crumpled his red cup. Probably pretending it was Todd's head. "I want to snap that guy in half."

"Pretty sure that would get us kicked out of the Battle," I said.

Hector shrugged. "Worth it."

"Forget him," Jared said, though he still glared in the direction Todd had gone. "We're going to win tonight, end of story."

"You mean, as long as Becca doesn't ditch us or pass out?" Hector asked.

"She'll be fine," I said and prayed I was right.

"Hey, who was that girl who gave you a ride?" Jared asked. "With the red hair?"

His question instantly put me on alert. "Why, you want to screw her, too?"

Jared arched an eyebrow at me. "No, I was just curious."

Hector snorted, and I looked at the ground, feeling like an ass. Maybe my question had been a bit harsh, but I was already pissed at my brother for everything else and the thought of him eyeing Alexis like one of his conquests made me crazy. And yeah, I had neglected to mention in my texts to Jared who I had gotten the ride from. I told myself it was because it hadn't seemed like the right time to bring it up with so much other shit going on, but mostly I didn't want to hear Jared give me a hard time about it. But I couldn't hide it from him forever.

"It was Alexis."

"No fucking way," Hector said, under his breath.

Jared stared at me, his mask slipping for an instant. "Alexis is here?"

"Yeah. I was shocked, too."

Hector shook his head. "Damn, she looks totally different. Nice car, though."

"She's not at Princeton?" Jared asked.

"No, she transferred to USC." I gave them both a quick rundown of the night so far, describing how Alexis had given me a ride and helped me find Becca, though I left out the part where we'd almost kissed. That was none of their business.

"Wow." Jared paced back and forth, like he had to walk this news off. "Alexis. I can't believe it. Why is she here? Oh, man, I bet she wants to get back together with you, doesn't she?"

I stared at the ground and said nothing.

He stopped in his tracks. "She *does*? What did you tell her?"

"I said I had to think about it."

"What is there to think about? Nothing. It's a bad idea. The end."

I knew he'd get on my case about this. He couldn't just trust me to make the decision on my own, like an adult. "Wow, thanks for the tip. But after this shit with Becca, I don't think you get to give me girl advice."

"He does have a point," Hector said to Jared.

Jared shot him a stay-out-of-this look and turned back to me. "That's different. Becca was a one-time mistake. Alexis is your Kryptonite. You need to stay away from her."

"He also has a point," Hector added to me.

I gave him an identical look to Jared's. "I'll figure this out, okay? I just need some time. But trust me, I know the risks.

Better than anyone."

Jared's face softened, and he wrapped an arm around my shoulder. "I'm sorry. I'm just trying to look out for you. I don't want you to get hurt again. But I know you'll sort it out."

"Thanks." I rubbed the all-black triangle on my wrist. Jared had been the one who put me back together after Alexis left the first time. I had finally gotten to a place where I could move on from her, but now she was back, tempting me again. A part of me wanted to give her another shot, to believe that this time would be different if I only gave her a chance, but I didn't know if Alexis had actually changed. Had I, really?

Jared touched the black triangle on his own wrist, and I knew he understood. After all, he'd had his own heart broken, too, by two of the people he'd trusted most. The tattoos were a reminder of what we'd been through together, of what we'd survived, of how—no matter what happened—we always had each other to rely on. As much as Jared drove me crazy, he did only want the best for me.

"Hey, what about your friend Maddie?" he asked. "Isn't she coming tonight? Maybe you should ask her out. Get out of your dry spell."

"We're not like that. We're just friends." Maddie was also a music major, and for all of freshman year, I'd had a thing for her. I'd sat beside her in every class we'd shared and made sure to get paired up with her on every duet or project. But I'd been too much of a chicken to do anything more. Alexis had taught me that good girls like Maddie weren't compatible with messed-up, tattooed guys like me. So I'd let it go. And over time, I'd realized Maddie and I were better as friends, anyway.

"You sure? 'Cause you talk about her all the time…"

"Seriously. We're friends. That's it." This wasn't the first time we'd had this conversation. He'd never met Maddie, but he was always telling me to go after her, like the "just friends" thing made no sense to him. As usual, Jared's advice involved thinking with his dick and not his head. I couldn't listen to any more of it. "I need a beer. I'll see you guys later."

The club had filled up a lot since I'd left, though the crowd thinned near the back around the bar. On stage, another band was playing bad heavy metal that made my ears bleed. I spotted Maddie at the edge of the crowd at the same moment she saw me, and I instantly felt a hundred times better at the sight of her smile. She wore a plaid shirt and jeans, her dark hair loose around her shoulders, her black-rimmed glasses framing her cute face.

She said something to the guy she was with—white button-up shirt, khaki shorts, and enough hair gel to be a fire hazard—and ran over to me. "There you are! I've been looking for you!" she yelled over the music.

"Hey, Maddie. Sorry, I ran out for a few minutes." I gave her a hug, and she felt nice in my arms but without the rush of desire that accompanied touching Alexis. Being with Maddie was easy, effortless, uncomplicated. If I was smart, I would have asked her out ages ago, like Jared had told me to, but it wasn't like that between us.

She grinned up at me. "This is so exciting! I can't wait to see you play."

"You've seen me play hundreds of times before," I said with a laugh.

"Not like this. Not with the whole band." She bounced on her heels a little. "You know I'm Villain Complex's biggest fan."

"You are. I'm really glad you're here."

I'd given her our album a few months ago. Our band had put it out ourselves once we'd had enough songs written. We'd rented a studio for a few hours to record them all, and then I'd done all the mixing and stuff in our home studio, while Jared had handled things like production and promotion. It had been the first time I'd used the skills I'd learned at school on our own music, and I'd worked hard to make it as good as possible. It meant a lot to me that Maddie, who was basically a musical prodigy, had approved of it.

I glanced behind her at Hair Gel Guy, who was playing on his phone. "Who's that with you?"

She looked back at him and sighed. "I'm on a date, but it's not going well."

"How come?"

"He already wants to leave. And he's just…boring."

"He can't be any worse than Chad." That was her last serious boyfriend. I'd had the urge to drive over to his place and smack some shit into him every time she'd mentioned what a dick he was.

"He's basically Chad 2.0." She adjusted her glasses. "Where's the rest of your band?"

"They're around here somewhere." As I said it, Jared appeared in the crowd, heading for the bar. I nodded in his direction. "Speak of the devil, there's my brother."

Maddie followed my gaze, and her eyes widened. "*That's* your brother?"

Oh, hell no. I'd seen that look a hundred times before. If this were a cartoon, little red hearts would be floating out of her eyes. She was caught in Jared's Death Star tractor beam, and there was no escape for her. That was exactly why I'd never introduced them before. I couldn't believe Maddie had succumbed so easily, too.

"That's him. Do you want to meet him?" *Please say no,* I thought.

"Oh, um…" Her cheeks flushed, making her look even cuter. "I should get back to my date. Maybe next time."

"Sure. Next time." Hopefully, there would be no next time. The last thing I wanted was for Jared to sleep with Maddie and leave me to deal with the fallout when he moved on the next day. Maddie was way too good for him, and I'd hate to have to strangle my brother. It's too bad, though, because if Jared wasn't such a prick, they'd be perfect for each other. They both lived and breathed music like it was a fundamental part of them, written into their very DNA. It was all so easy for them, too. I didn't have that gift, and I'd always envied them for that.

"I'll see you in class on Monday," she said. "Don't forget we're doing that piece from *The Dark Knight* score. And good luck tonight!"

We hugged again, and with a lingering gaze at Jared, she slipped back through the crowd to rejoin her date. I prayed she hadn't fallen under my brother's spell already. Maybe Chad 2.0 would turn out not to be a total loser. I doubted it, though. He didn't even glance up from his phone when she returned. What a punk.

Maddie didn't look back at me. Or at her date. No, she looked at my brother one last time. Just like every other girl, Maddie wanted the bad boy. She'd never once looked at me like that. No girl had…except Alexis. But even she'd said I was being too nice earlier. Her words replayed in my head: *Maybe it's time to be not so nice for a change.*

She was right. What had being nice gotten me, anyway? Nothing. Jared got all the girls, and I was forever alone. But the girl I wanted was here somewhere in the club, waiting for me. I just had to find the courage to go after her.

Screw it. Being the good guy had never worked out for me all these years. It was time to take a chance, to be more like my brother, to do something stupid for once.

It was time to be a little bad.

CHAPTER NINE

Alexis stood alone in front of the bar, watching the band on stage. Her leather jacket had been left in her car, and in her tight jeans and tiny, V-necked top, she radiated a cool, sexy confidence I found irresistible. She'd had that same confidence when we were younger, too, but now it had an edge, like she wasn't afraid to be herself. It made me want her even more.

I moved behind her, fitting myself against her back, and whispered her name in her ear. I didn't need to say anything else. She turned her head and met my eyes with a look of desire that matched my own. Her hand reached up to circle my neck, drawing my head down to hers, and I gave in to her siren call.

Our lips touched for the first time in three years. It was everything I remembered and more. Like waking from a long coma. A bright sunrise over a dark sky. The first hint of spring after a long winter. I was truly living again, in the way I normally only felt when I was on stage.

The kiss started slow, an awakening, an exploration, a forgiveness of our past mistakes. I teased at her mouth with my own, opening her wider, wanting more, wanting everything. Her lips were amazingly soft and sweet, like candy I'd tasted long ago and had finally rediscovered. I wrapped my arms around her hips, holding her flush against me. She groaned and dug her fingers into the back of my hair, pulling me even closer.

She turned in my arms to face me. "I guess this means you're giving me a second chance."

"I guess it does." I lowered my lips to hers again.

Our bodies fit together perfectly, like when we'd hugged except this time we didn't hold back. I slid my hands down to cup her butt, pressing her against the front of my jeans. Our kiss deepened, mouths hungry for each other, bodies desperate to be together again. We couldn't get close enough, couldn't get enough of each other. She clung to me like I was her savior, and I kissed her harder, flicking my tongue across hers, nibbling at her lower lip. Her fingers gripped the top of my jeans and tugged on them, like she wanted them gone. If she kept this up, I would rip her clothes off and take her right there on the bar counter.

This was all moving so fast, but I didn't care. This was exactly the kind of thing my brother did, and after being apart from Alexis for so long, I didn't want to go slow.

"Let's go to my car," she said, breathless. "The backseat…"

"My thoughts exactly."

We broke apart, and the rest of the club came into focus again. The crowd pressing around us in the dark. The clink of bottles behind the bar. The music blasting from the speakers. The lights illuminating the band on stage. I checked the time. About an hour before our set. No one would miss me if I slipped out for a few minutes.

I took Alexis's hand, the action so familiar I could almost believe we'd never broken up. She gave me a knowing smile and let me lead her through the club, weaving between other couples and head-banging fans. I couldn't get us out of there fast enough. My brain had shut off and my body had taken over, with only lust and primal urges controlling me now.

This might only last one night. I didn't care. I'd take one night with Alexis. As long as I reminded myself it was just sex and nothing more, I'd be fine. If Jared could do it, so could I.

Alexis slid her hand up my arm, pressing her body against my side as we walked, and all rational thought disappeared again— except for one warning flashing through my head, reminding me that I didn't have any condoms. We had some in the van, but the van was gone.

I stopped and turned to Alexis. "Wait. Do you have a condom?"

Her eyebrows jumped up. "That's a bit presumptuous of you."

Oh, shit. I was the biggest ass in the entire world. I was literally the worst guy ever. "I'm sorry, I'm such an idiot. I didn't…um, I just thought…"

She laughed and nudged me with her hip. "I'm kidding! We totally need a condom. Or five."

A slow grin spread across my face. "We don't have *that* much time before my set…"

"For later, then."

There was going to be a later? Now I couldn't *wait* to get to her car. "Give me one minute."

She gave me a long, lingering kiss that I didn't want to break away from. "I'll meet you at the car."

I found Jared backstage, sipping a beer and staring off into space. For once, he was alone. Where were all his groupies? He looked so lost in thought I almost hated to disturb him, but he snapped out of it when he saw me. "Hey, Kyle."

"Hey." I leaned close to him, lowering my voice. "I, uh…" Damn, this was embarrassing. I'd never had to ask my brother for this before. "I need some condoms."

His eyebrows show up. "You need some right now?"

"Um…yeah."

He laughed and wrapped an arm around my shoulders, yanking me close. "No way! Who's the lucky girl?"

"It's not that big a deal," I muttered, pulling away from him. It wasn't *that* rare for me to get laid.

"I'm just proud." But then his grin faded away. "Hang on. Who *is* the lucky girl?"

"Alexis." I stared him down, preparing for another lecture. I already knew everything he would say, and I didn't care. Yes, it was a mistake. Yes, I might get my heart broken again. Yes, I knew the risks.

Yes, I wanted to do it anyway.

But the lecture never came. Jared reached into the inside pocket of his leather jacket and yanked out a long strip of condoms. Way more than I would ever need tonight. Could he possibly use all those in one evening? No wonder he was so popular with women.

"Just be careful," he said.

"You gave me plenty of condoms for that."

"Not what I meant." He shook his head and opened his mouth like he wanted to say more, to give me older brother advice that I'd likely ignore, but then he seemed to change his mind. "Have fun."

"Thanks."

I shoved the condoms in my jeans and headed for the exit, but just outside the door, I was stopped by Todd. He moved in front of me, trying to block my path.

"Emo boy," he said. "Where you running off to?"

"None of your business." I didn't have time for his shit. I brushed past him, but he grabbed my arm hard.

He smirked, digging his fingers into my skin. "Almost time

for us to go on. You ready to get your ass handed to you?"

I yanked my arm away. "Fuck off, Todd."

He got right up in my face. "You think you're so fucking cool, with your tattoos and your black clothes, but you're not. You're a loser, and tonight I'm going to prove it to everyone."

He started laughing, like his words were hilarious, and I had that urge to rip his head off again. When I was in middle school, kids like him had bullied me because I'd been the weird, scrawny kid who always wore black and didn't really talk to anyone. Jared had always defended me, and now I made a fist the way he'd once taught me.

"Get out of my way."

"You're *all* losers," he went on, like he hadn't heard me. "Like Hector. He should be mowing my lawn, not playing drums. And Jared? He's the biggest loser of them all. He works as a bartender! Talk about a waste of a college education."

That was it. I could put up with him talking shit about me, but once he'd brought the other guys in, it was over. I'd ignored all his other crap this evening, but I'd had enough. Normally, I'd walk away or try to smooth things over. Good guys didn't get in fights.

Unfortunately for Todd, I'd just decided to stop being a good guy.

I slammed my fist into his eye. It hit with a loud *smack*, and pain shot through my hand. It'd probably be harder for me to play keyboard tonight, but it was worth it to see Todd stagger back, clutching his pretty-boy face.

"You son of a—" Todd lunged for me but stopped when Hector appeared at my side.

"You don't want to do that," Hector growled, the muscles in his arms flexing.

Todd stood up straighter, holding one hand over his eye. "Whatever. It's almost time for my set, anyway. I'll deal with you two later."

He stalked off, and Hector snorted. "Coward."

"Where did you come from?" I asked as I massaged my hand and stretched out my fingers.

He gestured across the parking lot. "I was sketching over there when I heard you two arguing. Nice shot, by the way."

"Thanks." I'd thought about hitting Todd many times before but had always stopped myself. Somehow that only made it sweeter now.

"I'm just sad I didn't get to punch him myself."

"Don't worry, there's still time."

He grinned and slapped me on the back. "You okay?"

"I'm good." My hand hurt and I was a little shaky from the adrenaline, but that would wear off soon. Mostly I just felt *alive*.

I could get used to this being-bad thing.

CHAPTER TEN

Alexis had parked at the very end of the lot under a broken streetlamp, giving us a tiny bit of extra privacy. She sat on the hood of her MINI, leaning back with one foot propped on the front bumper, and a rush of lust flooded me at the sight. She crooked a finger at me, beckoning me to her.

I took Alexis in my arms and kissed her like I was making up for all the years we'd been apart. Her nails grazed up my arms, along my tattoos, and she kissed me back even harder, like she needed to show me how much she regretted leaving me. And with my lips I showed her that I forgave her, that I wanted this as much as she did.

For tonight, at least, she was mine again. I wanted to taste every inch of her.

I started with her neck, kissing my way down the smooth, pale skin. I stopped just below her ear, focusing on a spot that had always driven her wild. She moaned and leaned back against the hood, pulling me down against her, spreading her legs around me. I loved hearing her make those noises, knowing I did that to her. I loved feeling her body underneath mine again.

I dipped lower, kissing along her collarbone, down the V of her shirt, across the top of her soft breasts. She gripped my hair hard, holding me to her chest, and for once, I was thankful I'd let it grow so long. I wanted to yank her top off, but we were still out in the open, where anyone could see us. Not that I cared much at the moment.

I moved back up to claim her lips and slipped a hand under her shirt. She gasped against my mouth as I slid my fingers across her smooth stomach up to her lacy bra, cupping each breast in my palm and tracing her nipples through the fabric. She arched up, legs wrapping around me, drawing me closer, grinding her body against my hips.

Her little, breathless cries did more to turn me on than she could ever know. I was harder than I'd been in years, practically bursting through my jeans to get to her. Her hands slid down to finger my studded belt, like she knew what I needed. She undid the buckle, and it made a soft *clank* as it hit the hood. Then she reached for my jeans, popping them open, relieving a little pressure there.

Someone whooped behind us, and we froze. I lifted myself off Alexis and glared at the two guys walking past, ogling us like they'd never seen two people making out on the hood of a car before.

Alexis slipped out from under me. For a second, I worried those guys had ruined our night together, but then she opened the car door and climbed into the backseat.

"You coming?" she asked in a teasing voice.

I grinned at her. "Soon, I hope."

She laughed, and I followed her inside. The backseat of the MINI was bigger than you'd expect from the outside, but there still wasn't a lot of room to move around in. At least the windows were tinted, giving us some privacy. I sat beside her on the dark leather seats but hesitated. This wasn't my style, hooking up with someone for a quickie in the back of a car.

But this wasn't some random girl I'd just met in the club. This was *Alexis*. We'd been each other's firsts. We'd learned how to please other people by practicing on each other. I knew her, inside and out—or, at least, I had once. I wanted to know her again, in every sense of the word.

"If we're going too fast..." she started, her face etched with concern.

"No," I said. "I want this. I want you."

"Good." She put her hands on my jaw and pulled me to her, kissing me hard. And just like that, my brain shut off again.

I gripped the hem of her top and yanked it off her. My eyes devoured her delicate, bare shoulders, her chest rising and falling with each breath, and that lacy bra teasing at what was underneath. God, she was the sexiest girl I'd ever seen. But that bra had to go.

I unhooked it and tossed it into the front seat. Her breasts were even more beautiful than I remembered, round and lush, with large, taut nipples just begging for me to suck on them. I cupped them in my hands and kissed each one, using my mouth and tongue to make her sigh. I knew what she liked, what drove her mad with pleasure, what made her gasp and cry my name. And I did it all.

"Kyle," she pleaded and tugged on my shirt.

I released her and sat back, letting her take over. She pulled my shirt off, and her eyes swept over me, taking in the sight of my inked skin, of everything that had changed since she'd last seen me. Her lips quirked up in a smile, and I knew she approved.

She leaned forward and kissed me again, her bare breasts crushing against my naked chest. I wrapped my arms around her, and she moved onto my lap, straddling me. I loved the feel of her like this, her skin against mine. Now if only our jeans weren't in the way.

Her lips brushed across my neck, along the flames and waves

dancing along my skin, and up to my earlobe. She traced the round black gauge with her tongue, and I dug my fingers into her hips to steady myself as twangs of hot pleasure shot through me.

"These are new," she whispered. "I like them."

She took my earlobe into her mouth and sucked, and I thought I might pass out from the sensation. And then she repeated it with the other ear, and I nearly did.

"Alexis," I groaned, but she didn't stop. Her mouth moved to my shoulders, to kiss the tattoos on my arms and chest, and finally to the small metal rings through my nipples. She dipped a finger through each, tugging a little, and I gasped.

"These are new, too." She flicked my nipple and the piercing with her tongue, and I cried out, nearly jolting out of the seat. "Oh, I *love* these."

I couldn't handle any more of this. I needed her, naked and sweating and on top of me. We didn't have much time, but even if we had all night, I didn't think I could wait any longer. Not after being apart so long.

She must have had the same thought because she started yanking at my jeans. I let her have at it, watching the way her red hair fell over her face as she tugged my clothes down. Not all the way off, but enough to get the job done. Then she shimmied her own jeans down, followed by pink lacy panties that matched her bra. I watched with hungry eyes and couldn't stop myself from touching her. I slid my hands along her shapely legs and up her thighs, but she pushed me back in the seat, taking charge again.

She climbed onto my lap, her knees on either side of my hips, rubbing herself against me. I looked up at her, pushing the hair away from her face. This was our last chance to back out of this, but I saw in her eyes that she wanted it as much as I did.

"Condom," I said, my voice strained. "In my jeans."

She grabbed one and ripped it open with her teeth, and wow, that was hot. She rolled it over me herself, her deft fingers working quickly but making me moan at the same time. She was much better at that than I remembered. How many guys had she been with since me, anyway? I pushed the thought away as she got the condom on and squeezed once, sending throbbing pleasure through me.

"Keep that up and I won't last long," I said through gritted teeth.

She laughed and placed her hands on my shoulders. I gripped her hips as she moved over me and then slid down, down, down, taking me in so slowly I thought I would die from the delicious agony of it. I filled her completely, her body sheltering me inside her. It was like coming home, and for a moment, neither of us moved, just enjoying the feeling of being one again. This was where we belonged: together.

"Kyle," she whispered. "I've wanted this for so long."

"Me too," I said into her red hair. It was so good I wanted to cry out, to shout to the heavens, to scream it across the parking lot.

She began to move, slowly at first, rocking over my hips, gliding up and down. Our mouths met again, our tongues dancing together, our lips sucking on each other. Her breasts rubbed against my chest as she increased her speed, and I groaned. I loved letting her take over like this, letting her be in control, letting her find her own pleasure.

I dug my fingers into her hips, urging her on as she pulsed on top of me. One of her hands pressed against the window of the car, leaving an imprint in the steam we'd created. She moved faster and faster, her movements growing wilder, and it was hard not to explode inside her. But I held back, focusing on pleasing her first.

I took each of her nipples in my fingers and teased them, and she rode me harder, bucking like a cowgirl, losing control. Her hands moved up to the ceiling, steadying herself as she angled her hips so I went even deeper. I clutched her back, helping her along, lifting my own hips to thrust into her.

Just when I thought the pleasure was too much and I couldn't hold back any longer, she cried out and closed her eyes, tightening around me. Feeling her body tremble, watching her face as she lost herself, it was too much for me. I let go, shuddering as I spilled myself into her, giving myself up to her completely.

She collapsed against me, and I held her close while we caught our breath. As our heartbeats slowed, I touched her cheek, stroking her soft skin. It was hard to believe she was really here with me, after so long. Being with Alexis was even better than I'd remembered, and there was no point fighting my feelings for her. I was already too far gone.

She took my hand and kissed each of the letters tattooed across my knuckles, spelling out the word *LIVE*. She went to kiss the *LOUD* on the other hand, but I flinched. It was still sore from punching Todd.

"You okay?" she asked.

"Yeah. I hurt my hand earlier. It's nothing. Don't worry." I pulled her close again and kissed her, hoping she'd drop it. I wasn't ashamed of punching Todd or anything, but I didn't want to bring it up with her, either. I had a feeling she'd be disappointed, even though she seemed to like the badder, bolder me.

When the kiss ended, she stroked my stubble and smiled. "I never thought.... I mean, I hoped this would happen. But I wasn't sure you'd ever take me back."

Me either, but I'd been deluding myself thinking I'd be fine with just one night together. "Alexis, I can't make any promises. I still need some time to figure things out." I paused, tracing her lips with my thumb. "But I do want to give this a shot."

"Oh, Kyle." She buried her face in my neck, resting against me, and for a few minutes, we just held each other. I'd missed Alexis so much and been heartbroken for so long, but that was over. Time and distance may have kept us apart, but we were together again...and maybe this time it would last.

CHAPTER ELEVEN

We returned to the club only minutes before Todd's band went on stage, and the place had filled up so much we had to squeeze our way through the crowd to get a good view. My band was up next and I had to find the others soon, but I wanted to check out our competition first. Plus, I was curious if Todd had a black eye already.

"Perfect timing," Alexis said, adjusting her camera. "I need to get photos of Rubber Horse's set."

"I thought that was just an excuse to come to the show tonight."

"Yes and no. I don't have an official assignment, but I did promise to take photos of them for their website."

Did that mean she was friends with them? Or was she just doing them a favor? I hated the idea of her doing anything for Todd and his entourage. Hell, I hated the idea of him even talking to her.

They walked out on stage in their pastel shirts and boat shoes, and Alexis cheered. Not just polite cheering with the rest of the crowd, either, but loud, arms-in-the-air, full-out-rooting-for-their-band kind of cheering. Like she was a Rubber Horse fangirl or something.

"What are you doing?" I asked, horrified.

She peered through her lens at the stage. "What do you mean?"

"Forget it." I shouldn't blame her for cheering for a USC band since she went there and all, but a bad feeling seated itself in my gut that I couldn't shake off.

Alexis gasped. "Oh, his eye! Did someone hit him? And now he has to play like that. Poor guy."

He did have a shiner over half his face, which made me a little proud. Jared had taught me well. But Alexis was acting like she was actually concerned about Todd. "Are you friends with him or something?"

"Yeah, I've known him since we were kids. Our parents are good friends. Now that I'm at USC, we hang out sometimes."

That explained it. One of her friends from that other part of her life that had never included me. I bet they played golf together and hung out on their families' boats wearing nautical-themed pashminas. Even though the thought made me want to set fire to something, I knew I should drop it. It wasn't my business who she was friends with or which band she cheered for. Even if it *was* Todd.

But then he grabbed his bass and flashed that cocky smirk, and I couldn't let it go.

"How can you be friends with a guy like that?"

She shrugged. "Once you get past the frat boy clothes, he's not so bad."

"Are you kidding me? Todd once asked Hector if he swam here from Mexico!"

"He said that?" She frowned, eyeing me closely. "Hang on—how do you even know him?"

"Todd was our bassist for a while, but Jared kicked him out."

"Ah," she said, like that explained everything.

"What?" I asked. She didn't answer, and that made me even more annoyed. "No, seriously, what was that 'ah' about?"

"Just that it makes sense now why you hate him."

"I hate him 'cause he's a dick!"

She rolled her eyes. "No, you hate him because Jared hates him. And Jared hates him because he's not Ben."

I stared at her, trying to make sense of her words. "That's ridiculous. We kicked Todd out because he's an asshole. End of story."

"He's not an asshole! He's kind of an idiot sometimes, but he's not that bad, really."

"Are we talking about the same Todd? The one on stage right now? Holding the bass?"

She propped her hands on her hips. "Kyle, I've been following your band all these years. I know you've been through a lot of bassists. No one will ever be good enough for Jared, not after Ben betrayed him, and you always go along with whatever Jared does because Ben was your best friend and you feel guilty. Admit it—this isn't about Todd at all."

"You've been gone for *three years*! You have no idea what we've been through in that time!" People around us were starting to stare, but I didn't care. Alexis was wrong. Yes, maybe I'd felt guilty about Ben once, but that was years ago. And maybe we'd gone through a ton of bassists, but only because they did shit like never showing up for practice or stealing money from us. We'd had bad luck, that's all.

"I know enough," she said. "I know you still look at guys like Todd and judge them without giving them a fair chance, just like you always did."

I took a step back, her words stinging. She was accusing *me* of caring about image? After she'd dumped me for not fitting into her life? After admitting she had changed her look to stop hiding who she was? Yes, I'd judged Todd, but on his words and his actions, not on anything else. How could she not see the real him? He must have her completely fooled.

Or maybe she just didn't *want* to see it.

I was about to argue with her, but Rubber Horse started playing and the music blasting from the speakers drowned out any words I might say. The worst part was they were pretty good. They sounded sort of like Sublime or 311, a mellow stoner jam with a hint of reggae, and they even had a white-boy rapper. Not my kind of music, but they made it work.

Alexis snapped photos as they played, and I realized nothing had changed between us. Yes, she looked different and she'd come back to LA, but underneath she was still the girl who hung out with guys like Todd and then sneaked off with guys like me to hook up in the back of cars. I couldn't go through that again.

"Be honest. Who do you want to win tonight?" I asked, yelling over the music.

Her mouth dropped open. "That's not fair! I go to USC and they're my friends, too—"

That said it all. "I figured. God, this is just like Princeton all over again."

"What's that supposed to mean?"

"You choosing your perfect, father-approved friends over me, just like before. It will never end, will it?"

She huffed. "I'm not choosing them over you! I want *both* of your bands to win!"

"But only one of us can!" I shook my head, and my hair fell in front of my eyes. I pushed it out of my face, and Alexis caught my hand, making me yelp.

Her eyes widened. "Oh my god, you're the one who hit him!"

I rubbed it, trying to smooth out the ache. "Trust me, he deserved it."

"For what? For not fitting into your scene? For saying something you didn't like? I can't believe you'd do that!"

"*I* can't believe you're taking his side!"

"I'm not taking his side!"

"You don't know what he's like! He's been harassing me and the other guys all night. He—"

"I don't care what he did! That's not who you are! Or, at least, that's not the Kyle *I* used to know. That Kyle was a good guy. Not the kind of guy who went around punching people he didn't like." She sucked in a long breath. "I'm sorry. I just… I'm not sure I like this new version of you."

As the song ended, she stared at me like she'd never seen me before, like I was a stranger, and that hurt more than anything. Maybe I'd been wrong to hit Todd, but she wouldn't even listen to me explain why I'd done it. No matter what I said, I would never be good enough for Alexis and she would never be on my side.

"This was a mistake," I said.

"What do you mean?"

"You and me." I tried not to let my voice shake, hiding how hard it was to say those words. "It's never going to work. We tried but…we're just too different."

"But…" Her lip trembled, and she looked away. "Maybe you're right."

The next song started, and she turned back to the stage to take another photo. I'd expected her to fight harder, to beg me to change my mind, but maybe she'd realized we were still as messed up as we'd always been. If we couldn't make it through one night without fighting, what kind of chance did we have for the future?

There was nothing else to say. I left her there, letting the crowd swallow me up, just another tattooed guy in black. A guy who'd just walked away from the only woman he'd ever loved.

CHAPTER TWELVE

Jared found me outside, sitting on the ground against the side of the club. He sank down beside me, and for a few minutes, we watched the palm trees blow under the handful of visible stars in the LA night sky.

Finally, he broke the silence. "I really fucked things up, didn't I?"

It took a second for me to realize he was referring to the Becca drama. I'd been so wrapped up in my own screw-up, I'd momentarily forgotten about it. "We all do stupid things sometimes."

"Yeah, but I'm the only one who nearly ripped the band apart." He ran a hand through his hair, his telltale, stressed-out move. "We're going to lose another bassist, and it's all my fault."

"If that happens, we'll deal with it. And it's not entirely your fault. Becca's partly to blame, too."

"No, I really screwed up this time." He leaned his head against the wall and closed his eyes. "I can't keep doing this, Kyle. I can't keep being this guy. I need to get my shit together."

I hated seeing him like this. This Jared was different from the one on stage, the one all his groupies saw. Even though he acted the part of the bad boy, deep down he was a good guy, too. Problem was he didn't believe it himself. As much as I wished he would go back to the old Jared, I wasn't sure he ever would. He enjoyed being the villain too much.

I draped an arm across his shoulders. "Hey, it's going to be okay. We'll figure it out."

"Yeah." He slumped against me. "What happened with Alexis?"

I picked at a tiny hole in my jeans, debating how much to tell my brother. "I messed everything up with her. We, uh, hooked up and I thought things were going well, but then I punched Todd. Turns out he's one of her friends."

"You punched Todd?" He laughed. "Well, I'm sure he deserved it."

"Exactly! I tried to tell her that, but she wouldn't listen."

Except...Todd hadn't *really* deserved it. He'd insulted the band, but I didn't care what Todd thought about us. He'd grabbed my arm and gotten in my face, but I should have walked away. I should have let it go.

"You were doing the world a service," Jared said. "I wanted to punch him myself for that terrible Bob Marley cover his band did."

"I must have left before that."

He shuddered. "Trust me, it was painful. You don't mess with a classic like that."

"I shouldn't have punched him. I let him get to me. It was stupid."

He elbowed me. "Hey, what did you just tell me? We all do stupid things sometimes."

Except, I wasn't allowed to do stupid things. I was the one who was supposed to have it together. Jared was our leader, the mastermind who wrote most of the music and took care of the management stuff the rest of us didn't have time for. Hector was the one who challenged Jared on his bullshit, the rock who was always there to support us through everything. And I was the mediator, the one who held us all together, who smoothed things over and fixed our problems. I couldn't afford to make mistakes, not when the other guys were counting on me.

"Don't be like me, Kyle," Jared said. "Quick hook-ups in cars, punching people…. That's not you. You're better than that."

I dropped my head. His words hit a little too close to home. I'd been so hung up on being "bad" that I'd forgotten who I really was. I'd thought I had to be more like my brother to get the girl. I'd thought Alexis wanted me to be that kind of guy. But I was wrong. She'd loved me for who I was.

I'd blown it with her, but maybe that was for the best. Did I want to be with someone I didn't trust not to break my heart again? Who hung out with guys like Todd? I wasn't sure.

I sighed. "You were right. I should have stayed away from Alexis."

"No, *you* were right. I'm the last person who should give relationship advice." Jared toed a rock with his boot. "All these years you've never gotten over Alexis, and now you have a chance to start over with her. You have to try. Just talk to her again."

"I don't know. Maybe we're too…broken."

"You're not broken, just…bent. Like that P!nk song with the guy from fun."

He started singing "Just Give Me a Reason," and I jabbed him in his side. "Stop that."

"Sorry," he said. "Seriously, though. She's here and she wants you back. She even helped you find Becca. So she has bad taste in friends. No one's perfect. But isn't she worth fighting for?"

I wasn't sure why Jared had changed his mind about Alexis, but maybe I should listen to him for once. I hadn't exactly given her a real chance tonight. I'd made a mistake by punching Todd, but instead of owning up to it, I'd used it as an excuse to end things with her. All because I was scared of getting hurt again.

But if I continued this way, I'd never open myself up to

anyone. Alexis was my first love. My *only* love. She was worth fighting for.

I stood up and brushed off my jeans. "Thanks for the pep talk. I'll go find her."

"Any time." He checked his phone. "But it'll have to wait. We only have ten minutes before our set."

We hurried backstage to where our gear was being stored. Hector was already there, waiting. "About time," he said. "Where's Becca?"

Oh, shit. Not this again.

"She's not here?" I glanced around the backstage area. All of the other bands had already performed and were in the main part of the club, so it was nearly empty. No sign of Becca's blue hair anywhere.

"I haven't seen her since you came back with her," Hector said.

Jared frowned. "Me either."

"We still have a few minutes," I said. "She'll show up." *Please show up, Becca.*

Hector took off his Villain Complex hat, raked his hand through his curly hair, and shoved it back on again. "And if she doesn't?"

I didn't need to answer because we all knew what would happen. We couldn't play without a bassist. Okay, technically we could, but it wouldn't sound right. We might as well hand the prize to Todd right now.

"Let's start setting up," I said. "If she's not here in the next five minutes, we'll…figure something out."

As I said it, Todd and his band walked off stage, carrying their gear and laughing. They stopped and glared when they saw us, their laser beam eyes seeming to hone in on me. I didn't blame them for being pissed at me for punching their bassist. I'd be pretty mad, too, if I was in their shoes. But this could only lead to trouble.

"There you are." Todd set down his guitar case and cracked his knuckles. "Payback time."

"We're a little busy at the moment," Jared said, hefting his own case. "Rain check, maybe?"

"Looks like the perfect time to me." Todd and his entourage moved closer, like sharks circling in for the kill. "If you're too fucked up to play afterward, not our problem."

How nice of Todd to pick the moment right before our set to try to beat us up. We were outnumbered, but Hector counted as at least two guys on his own, which evened it out. Our two bands stared each other down, like cowboys about to get into a shootout. We were all tense and ready to reach for our guns, but no one wanted to make the first move. I almost expected a tumbleweed to roll past us.

Hector smacked his fist into his other palm. "Bring it on."

"Wait." I couldn't let our bands fight each other over my one lapse in judgment. Jared and Alexis were both right—that wasn't who I was.

I wasn't that kind of guy. I wasn't like my brother. But maybe that wasn't a bad thing.

Besides, we didn't have time for this shit.

"I'm sorry I hit you, Todd. I've been having a rough night, and I took it out on you. It was inexcusable, and I apologize."

Todd blinked, and then he burst out laughing. I thought we might be okay until it turned into a mocking kind of laugh.

"Damn, it's going to feel even better when I pound your face in after that pathetic speech." A wide, evil grin spread across his face. "You know, I saw you with Alexis earlier. But she's coming home with me tonight 'cause you're such a pussy. And when I'm balls-deep in her, it'll be even sweeter knowing I'll have won the Battle *and* the girl."

He laughed again, and Jared took a step forward, fists clenched. I put a hand on his arm to stop him. The thought of Todd sleeping with Alexis made me want to punch him again, to beat him until he couldn't move—let alone *think* of touching her—but I wouldn't let him get to me this time.

I shrugged, like his words didn't affect me at all. "She can go home with whoever she wants, but hey, how about I buy you all a round of drinks after the show? What do you guys think?"

His eyes narrowed, like he didn't understand why I wasn't coming at him, fists flying. The other guys in his band looked confused, too.

"I could go for a drink," the rapper said, and the others nodded.

"No." Todd got up in my face again and poked a finger in my chest. "We're settling this right here, right now."

Well, I'd tried. I really had. But being nice to Todd only seemed to make him angrier, and Becca was still MIA. If we weren't going to perform tonight, we might as well go out with a bang. I sucked in a breath and readied myself. I wouldn't throw the first punch this time, but I wasn't going to let him beat the shit out of me either.

"Kyle was right about you, Todd," Alexis said from behind me. "You *are* an asshole."

I spun around at the sound of her voice. She glared at him like she might shoot fire from her eyes and burn him down where he stood. Becca was at her side, her arms crossed. They looked like they could take on all four guys themselves.

"Hey, baby," Todd said, flashing Alexis his pretty-boy smile. "You know I was just joking about all that. You're still coming to my party tonight, right?"

"No, I'll be celebrating with Villain Complex after *they* win."

"Huh?" His face twisted, shifting from surprise to anger. "You're going to pick these losers over us?"

"I am," she said. "And I suggest you get out of here before I tell the guy running this show what's holding up the final band."

Alexis moved to stand beside me and flipped her red hair over her shoulder, looking like some kind of warrior princess ready to do battle. God, I loved this woman.

Todd's buddies hesitated, dropping their shoulders, backing

off. Maybe because they didn't want to have to fight a girl. Maybe because they were outnumbered now. Or maybe I'd appealed to their decent sides earlier and they were starting to question if listening to Todd was such a good idea.

"Let's go," one of them said. The rest agreed, and they took off down the hallway, grabbing their gear as they went. Todd growled at us, but after one final look of pure hatred directed at me, he turned on his heel and followed.

As soon as they were gone, we all seemed to collectively relax, the tension vanishing from the air. My brother turned to Alexis and pulled her in for a hug. "It's good to see you again."

"You too, Jared." I detected a little quiver in her voice as she hugged him back. He whispered something to her that I didn't catch, but she bit her lip and nodded.

Hector brought her in for a big bear hug next. "Damn, it's been a long time, girl."

"Yay, we're all best friends again," Becca said, rolling her eyes. "Can we get on with the show already?"

"Oh, now you care?" Jared asked. "Where were you five minutes ago?"

"I was about to take off, but Alexis convinced me to stay," she said, glaring at him. "So let's do this before I change my mind again."

She grabbed her bass and stomped out to the stage. That one was a ticking bomb that I'd never be able to diffuse. At least for tonight, she was still part of the band—thanks to Alexis.

Jared and Hector grabbed their gear and headed after her. We were already running late, but I had to say something to Alexis before I could go.

I stared at her while a million emotions rushed through me at the speed of light. She'd convinced Becca to stay and had chosen me over Todd. She'd taken my side, and she was rooting for me to win. I just hoped she could forgive me for the things I'd said to her. I hoped she could see I was still the good guy she loved.

"Thank you," I said. "For Todd and for Becca and for being here tonight. And I'm sorry about earlier. I was totally out of line and—"

Alexis raised a hand to stop me. "No, I was the one who was out of line, and I'm sorry, too—"

"Kyle, come on!" Jared yelled.

She kissed me on the cheek. "Go out there and win this thing, babe. I'll be here when you're done."

I gave her a quick hug and then ran after the rest of my band. I wanted to do so much more—to kiss her and tell her how much she meant to me and how I wanted to start over—but there was no time. We had a Battle to win. Because no matter what else happened tonight, we were *not* losing to Todd.

CHAPTER THIRTEEN

Being on stage was unlike anything else in the world. Every show was a spiritual awakening, a moment of enlightenment when all my daily troubles faded away and left only the roar of the crowd and the lights and the music. Performing was magic, an act of creation that controlled the emotions of those who heard the music, forming a shared experience between everyone in the room.

And being part of a band—with each person contributing, harmonizing, and creating magic together—was a true rush. We weren't individuals anymore; we were one voice, one breath, one heartbeat. The only thing that came close was having sex, and even then, only those really good times or with the person who made it truly special. Like Alexis.

I knew she was out there in the audience somewhere, cheering for me, and that made the moment even better. Maddie was out there, too. My brother was at my side, and Hector was at my back. Even Becca had pulled it together. I was surrounded on all sides by people I cared about, and I channeled that energy into my performance.

My fingers flew across my keyboard, my head banging along to the music. Unlike other instruments, with keyboard, there was no specific role you took on for every song. Each one was different, and I filled in where I was needed—sometimes accentuating another instrument, sometimes adding something extra here and there, sometimes providing a background ambiance for the entire song. I brought together Jared's hard guitar riffs, Becca's pulsing bass line, and Hector's steady beat. I picked up the slack. I smoothed any rough spots. I held them together and boosted them up. They could have performed the songs without me, but I made each one a hundred times better.

Our set was only fifteen minutes, so we played the catchiest tunes off our album. In the middle, we did a cover of "Karma Police" by Radiohead, with Jared's vocals making the audience swoon. The song's lyrics struck a nerve with me tonight after everything I'd been through. I really had lost myself for a few minutes, but here on stage, with my favorite people all around me, I knew exactly who I was.

We finished the set with one of our best songs, "Behind the Mask." As the last note died, the crowd went wild and Jared spread his arms out as if to embrace them. The sound filled me up, sustaining me like air, and I closed my eyes and breathed it in. And then I ran backstage. I had a beautiful girl waiting for me, after all.

Her eyes lit up when she saw me. I walked right up to her, took her face in my hands, and kissed her. Her fingers dug into my shirt as she kissed me back, and I slid my arms down to circle her waist. My heart was already pounding from the show, but she made it speed up even more as her body pressed against mine and her tongue slipped into my mouth. I nibbled on her lower lip and felt her smile. The rest of the band walked off stage, but they wisely left us alone.

"You were amazing," she said, breathless. "You were always good, but now…it was epic."

"Thanks." I kissed her again. "But there wouldn't have been a show without you."

"I barely did anything." She ran her thumb across my jaw, her eyes fixed on the tattoos on my neck. "I'm sorry I didn't listen to you about Todd. I've never seen that side of him before, I swear. He's always been a decent guy around me, but I should have trusted you."

"No, you had every right to stick up for your friend. I'm the one who messed up. I shouldn't have punched him in the first place, and I shouldn't have used him as an excuse to pick a fight with you. I was just scared. I barely survived when you left me last time, and I'm terrified of going through the same thing a second time."

"I'm so sorry, Kyle. I thought if I ended it we would both be better off, but I was wrong. I'll never make that mistake again."

"No regrets," I said, brushing hair away from her face so I could stare into her green eyes. "As much as it hurt, being apart for three years was good for us. We've both grown and changed, and we'll be stronger together because of it. But I don't want to go another day without you."

"Good because I want to make it last this time. Whatever it takes." She slid her arms around my neck. "I love you, Kyle."

"Still?"

"Always."

We kissed again, losing ourselves in each other until Jared told us it was time for the audience to vote for a winner. The entire band, plus Alexis, rushed into the main part of the club, blending into the crowd and looking up at the stage. The Battle of the Bands organizer stood up there, an older guy who looked like he was straight out of an '80s metal band with hair down to his waist, an old AC/DC shirt, and leather pants.

"We're going to vote by school first," he said into his mic. "I have an app here on my phone that measures sound levels, so when we get to the band you think should win, scream your heart out. I want you to make some fucking noise!" The audience cheered in response. "Exactly like that. Okay, ready? USC first!"

He ran through the list of USC bands, with each name flashing on a screen behind him. Rubber Horse easily won, which didn't surprise me. What did surprise me was that Alexis didn't cheer for any of her school's bands.

The guy checked his phone. "Rubber Horse is our USC winner! And now it's time for UCLA!"

He called out each of the bands that had performed, and the sound from the crowd grew louder with each one. When the Villain Complex logo flashed on the screen, the audience's roar took over the room. We joined in, too, yelling and clapping, and it felt good to let it all out after everything I'd been through tonight.

It felt even better when the guy said, "Villain Complex is the UCLA winner!"

"Yes!" I gave Alexis a squeeze, and she laughed. Next to us, Jared and Hector were hugging and thumping each other on the back. Even Becca looked slightly less sullen than normal.

"Time for the final vote," the guy said. "Rubber Horse versus Villain Complex. USC vs UCLA. Only one of them can be crowned the winner of the Battle of the Bands and get the prize: a show next month, plus one thousand dollars for themselves and another thousand for their school's music program. Will USC win again for the third year in a row? Or will UCLA finally take it home?"

This was it. The moment we'd find out if everything we'd been through tonight had been worth it. Jared wrapped an arm around me and Hector, and I grabbed Alexis's hand. We tried to pull Becca in, too, but she rolled her eyes and crossed her arms.

The cheers for Rubber Horse were loud, but when our band's name was called out, the response from the audience was almost deafening. The club filled with the sound of the crowd voting for us with their voices and their bodies. Yelling. Clapping. Whistling. Stomping their boots. Alexis was part of it, screaming louder than anyone. I was too shocked by the reaction to even cheer for us myself. Jared's eyes met mine, and I could tell he felt the same.

"Villain Complex is the winner of the third annual UCLA vs. USC Battle of the Bands!"

We collapsed in on each other in one big group hug, laughing and shaking from the adrenaline, from the relief and exhilaration of victory. Becca even joined in this time. We'd done it. We'd beaten Todd, won the prize for our school, and scored a gig for ourselves at the same time. And we'd done it together, as one big, sometimes-dysfunctional, family. None of us could have done it without the other—and that included Alexis.

I pulled apart from the rest of the band and kissed her in the middle of the audience while they continued to cheer for our win. I would never forget this night, marking a fresh start and a new beginning. For the band, and for the two of us.

CHAPTER FOURTEEN

I woke with Alexis in my arms. I might have written last night off as a really great dream, except the proof that it was real slept beside me, wearing only my old Ramones T-shirt. Alexis was in my bedroom, her bare legs tangled up with mine, and we'd won the Battle. Every time it hit me, it felt too amazing to be true, like it must have happened to someone else and not me. But no, this was my life.

Alexis looked so beautiful. I wanted to kiss the freckles on her nose and breathe in the strawberry scent of her hair. Her half-naked body felt so good against mine I wanted to do more than just kiss her, but I let her be. I could save all of that for when she woke up. It was Sunday, and my plan was to spend the entire day with the girl I loved, learning her body all over again.

I slipped out of bed, careful not to disturb her, and threw on a pair of boxers. It was still early, barely past dawn, so I moved quietly through the house to get some water from the kitchen. I paused when I heard a noise coming from our garage-turned-studio. The room was soundproofed, but the door was open.

Inside, Jared was sprawled on the couch with his laptop, wearing a shirt with *Lex Luthor for President* on it. My brother was obsessed with villains, hence our band name. We even had a wall of quotes by and about villains on the wall above where he sat that Hector had painted for us in comic book style.

Seeing Jared awake before noon was a rare occurrence. Even more shocking, he hadn't brought a girl home with him last night. Maybe he *was* trying to get his shit together.

"What are you doing up this early?" I asked.

"Oh, hey," he said, looking up from his screen. "The show recorded all of the different sets last night and posted them online. I got the video, and I'm using it to apply for *The Sound*."

I rubbed my eyes, still not entirely awake. "The reality TV show?"

On *The Sound*, a bunch of different bands competed against each other on four teams led by famous musicians. The winning band got a recording contract with a major label, plus a tour across the country. It was a big deal, but thousands of bands auditioned for it every year. Our chances of getting on were pretty slim.

He nodded. "I know it's a long shot, but I don't see a reason not to try."

"Might as well." I didn't think anything would come of it, but it always made Jared feel better when he had something to do for the band. "We'll have to deal with Becca, though."

"I'll talk to her."

I started to argue that I should do it, but then I closed my mouth. Jared needed to start fixing his own problems. As much as I loved my brother, I couldn't clean up after him for the rest of his life.

I yawned. "I'm going back to bed."

Jared grinned at me, like he knew exactly what I had in mind for the rest of the day. "Have a good time."

I crawled into bed with Alexis, and she stirred, opening her eyes with a sleepy smile. We wrapped around each other, so close we were almost one person, and it was pure heaven having her in my arms again. She'd come back to me, and she still loved me, proving that sometimes the good guy *did* get the girl. We'd gotten a second chance, and this time we were going to make it last.

I touched the tattoo on her hip and kissed her, and her lips tasted like forever.

Will Jared ever change his ways and find love?
Turn the page to read the first chapter of the next book
in the series, *More Than Music*.

CHAPTER ONE

Tonight was going to be epic, I could feel it. I edged closer to the stage, pushing past emo kids with sweeping black hair and girls in fishnets and combat boots. Julie and Carla followed, our hands linked so we wouldn't lose each other while I searched for the perfect spot. Not right in front so we looked like obsessed groupies hanging all over the band, but close enough to get a good view of the stage and feel the music vibrating under our skin. After some maneuvering, the three of us wedged into a space in the crowd and clinked our beers together.

"Here's to the end of finals," Julie shouted, over the noise of a hundred conversations going on at once. "And the end of our junior year!"

"I still have a final tomorrow morning," Carla shouted back. "What time are they going on again, Maddie?"

"Any minute now," I said. "Don't worry. Kyle's band only has one album. We'll be out of here in an hour." I had a final early, too, and normally I'd be studying right now and then going to bed at a reasonable hour to make sure I got an optimal amount of sleep. But it wasn't every day a friend's band got a gig like this in a club on Hollywood Boulevard. Besides, I was a music major. This totally counted as research.

I rocked back and forth on my feet, full of that intoxicating mix of excitement, anticipation, and longing I always felt right before a concert started. The club was dark except for the spotlights highlighting the equipment on stage, poised and ready for the band to come out. People with dyed hair and tattoos and piercings pressed all around us, and I felt more out of place than ever with my black-rimmed glasses, red flannel shirt, and jeans.

Julie fit into the crowd better with her knit panda beanie, despite it being approximately the temperature of the sun in here. She'd made the hat herself and on anyone else it would look stupid, but with her long black hair and red lips, she somehow managed to pull it off. Combined with the skater dress with stars and planets that she'd also made, she was really rocking her sexy nerd look tonight. Sort of like an Asian version of Zooey Deschanel.

Carla looked gorgeous as usual, like she'd walked straight off the runway and into the club, which she probably had—she modeled on the side while pursuing her theatre major. She was half-Portuguese and half-African-American, and casting agencies went crazy for her smooth dark skin, head full of wild curls, and tall, thin frame. It was a shame Julie and I were the only ones who knew she'd rather fix old cars and play video games than do a photo shoot.

The glow of Carla's phone lit up her face as she checked her texts yet again. Probably another string of annoying questions from her boyfriend.

"Is that Daryl?" I asked.

"He just wants to know where I am."

"Don't tell him," Julie said, slapping the phone away. "He'll show up uninvited."

It wouldn't be the first time he'd crashed our girls' nights looking for Carla, convinced she was with some other guy. Probably because he knew she could do way better.

"He won't. I told him we're leaving right after the show."

A cheer went through the crowd as the band walked onto the stage, and I stood on my toes to get a better look. Hector, a Latino guy with curly hair tucked under a baseball cap, sat in front of the drums. He was followed by Becca, a blue-haired pixie in a dress with safety pins all over it. She stumbled across the stage like she was drunk, but managed to pick up her bass and slip it over her neck. Next came Kyle, his black hair hanging in his eyes and the gauges in his ear flashing under the lights. He moved behind his keyboard, but my gaze left him as soon as his older brother Jared appeared.

The crowd's cheering took on more of a screaming sound, and one girl even yelled, "Jared, I love you!" I rolled my eyes. Not that I blamed the girl. With dark hair that always stuck up like he'd just gotten out of bed, a perpetual five o'clock shadow, and blue eyes that could charm any girl into giving him his phone number, Jared was impossible to resist. I wanted to, believe me, but every time he opened his mouth and sang it was all over.

Jared gave the audience a wicked grin while he grabbed his guitar, a black Fender Stratocaster almost identical to my own except for the color. Like Kyle, he had tattoos running up and down his toned arms, and I couldn't help but wonder if they continued under his shirt.

The entire club buzzed with excitement, every one of us poised on the edge, holding our breaths and waiting for the plunge. In this moment, right before the music started, it felt like anything could happen—and I was ready.

Hector yelled out, "One, two, three, four," and the band launched into their first song. Jared's hard guitar riffs filled the small club, matched with the deep pulse of the bass, the fierce beat of the drums, and the eerie moan from Kyle's keyboard. The music ripped through me, touching the wild, dark part of my soul I kept locked away. My fingers itched to form the chords myself and play along, but I kept my hands in fists at my sides. Instead I nodded my head to the music, picking out each note Jared played and feeling it in a way only another musician could.

When Jared leaned into the mic and sang, his smooth voice washed over me like a soft caress. It was like the last, decadent bite of a chocolate-covered strawberry. The smoky burn of whiskey as it slipped down your throat. The final night of passion before your lover left forever. I sang along to the words, feeling each line strike me deep inside. I understood exactly what he was saying, like he'd written every word just for me, like somehow he understood me in a way no one else did. Of course, every other girl in the club probably felt the same way I did. And a few guys, too.

I tore my gaze from Jared to watch the rest of the band. Hector was a blur as his muscular arms flew across the drums. Becca swayed while she played bass, her movements sluggish and her eyes half-closed like she could barely keep herself awake. Lately Kyle had been complaining about how she kept coming to rehearsals wasted, but I couldn't believe she'd do that tonight, not for their biggest performance ever.

Kyle was bent over his keyboard, head bobbing along while he played, and I loved seeing him in his element. We'd met as freshmen, and since we were both music majors who played piano, we always ended up in a lot of the same classes. We didn't hang out much outside of school or anything, but whenever we had a group project or a duet to perform we always paired up. Over the years, we'd bonded over a shared love of movie scores, superheroes, and other geeky stuff, even though he was covered in tattoos and never wore anything other than black and I thought staying up past eleven was living on the edge. Somehow we'd just clicked—but never in a romantic way.

The song ended, and the audience cheered. Jared flashed the crowd a smile full of dark promises. "Thank you," he said. "We're Villain Complex."

Julie whistled loudly beside me, and Carla covered her ears from the piercing sound. I blinked at them, coming out of a fog. I'd been so lost in the music I'd completely forgotten my friends were with me.

"They're so good!" Carla yelled.

"And the guys are so hot!" Julie added.

"I told you!" I shouted back at them. And then the next song started and I was swept away, falling under Jared's spell again.

Villain Complex had won the UCLA vs USC Battle of the Bands a month ago, securing the win for UCLA and making Kyle an instant celebrity around campus. Before that they'd only done a handful of small gigs and parties, playing both covers and songs from their own self-produced album. They were so talented it was only a matter of time until they really took off, and I'd be able to say I knew them before they were famous.

When the show ended, most of the audience crushed toward the exit like a herd of sheep. I was one of the few people crazy enough to move against the crowd and head for the stage, losing Julie and Carla somewhere in the fray. I finally made it to the front, next to a bunch of groupies gazing at Jared while he bent over to unplug something. I struggled not to stare along with them, but was saved when Kyle spotted me.

"Maddie, you came!" He jumped off the stage and grabbed me in a hug.

"I wouldn't miss it for anything. You were amazing!"

"Yeah?" He brushed hair away from his face, the tattoos on his fingers spelling out LIVE LOUD. "I was so nervous. You have no idea."

"It was a great show. Seriously. I was impressed."

"Thanks. That means a lot, coming from you." His face broke out into a grin. "Hey, I didn't get a chance to tell you the news. We have a live audition for *The Sound* on Friday!"

"What? No freaking way!" *The Sound* was a reality TV show where different rock bands competed against each other while being mentored by a famous musician. The winning band got a recording contract with a major label, and the top four bands were sent on tour together across the country. Plus, the show had millions of viewers, so even the bands that didn't win picked up a ton of new fans just from being on it.

"I know. Crazy, right?" He laughed like he couldn't believe it himself. "Jared sent in a video of us performing, plus MP3s of all our songs and a bunch of other shit. I didn't think anything would happen with it, but yesterday a producer called out of the blue and invited us to come on the show to audition."

"Wow, this is huge! I'm so happy for you." I gave him another hug and meant every word I said—but I was prickling with a touch of envy, too. I wanted Kyle and his band to win, of course. And it's not like I wanted to go on *The Sound* or anything, hell no. It's just that, for once in my life, I'd like to do something bold like that, too. No more standing in the crowd and cheering for others, no more hiding in an orchestra or behind a piano, but on stage, living the dream out loud and in front. But that wasn't me.

A girl with hair the color of fruit punch slammed against Kyle, wrapping her inked arms around him. They kissed for the longest, most awkward moment ever while I stood next to them like a creepy voyeur. Finally they remembered I was there and broke away, grinning like two beautiful misfits in love.

"Hey, Maddie!" Alexis said with a big smile. "Wasn't Kyle incredible up there?"

"He really was," I agreed.

"I'm so proud of you, babe." She kissed his cheek, and he smiled at her like he was the luckiest guy in the world. They'd been high school sweethearts but had broken up when she'd gone to Princeton. Now that she'd transferred to USC, they'd reconnected at the Battle of the Bands and had been inseparable ever since.

"Hey, I got some killer photos of the show," she said. "I can't wait to get them on the website."

"Cool. Send them to Jared so he can put them up." He jerked his head toward his brother, who was talking with one of the groupies. "Jared!"

Uh oh. So far I'd managed to avoid all interactions with Jared for my own safety. Kyle had warned me that his brother had a new girl every week, and I knew they definitely weren't geeky girls like me. If we never met, then Jared could remain the version in my head, the guy who wrote songs that made me feel less alone in the middle of the night and who grinned at the audience like he knew their darkest secrets. Once we met, he would be a real person. But I couldn't exactly run off now, not with him walking over to us, even though the voice in my head yelled, *Go, go, go!*

"What's up?" Jared asked, smiling at us. It was a different smile from the one he used on stage, a private smile for friends that made him look even more like Kyle. I saw the real him for the first time, and it was even better than I'd imagined. I was doomed.

"Kyle talks about you all the time," Jared said to me, after we were introduced. "Great to finally meet you."

He hopped off the stage and spread his arms, moving in like he wanted to hug me. This wasn't all that shocking since Kyle was a hugger, too, but I stood there, frozen and tongue-tied for an excruciatingly long pause. It should be criminal for a man to be so good-looking. How were normal girls like myself supposed to touch the sun without getting burned?

"You too," I finally said and stepped toward him.

As his strong arms circled me, a little tremor ran through my body, like a static shock jolting right through my chest. He was the perfect height for me to press my face into the curve of his neck and breathe him in, but I restrained myself. The hug was brief, but even that second of contact was enough to leave me breathless. I quickly pulled away and took a few steps back to a safe distance.

"We're having a party at our place after this," Kyle said. "You should come, Maddie."

"Thanks, but I should get home." I had that final in the morning, and Carla would kill me if I kept her out all night. Besides, Kyle and I didn't exactly run in the same crowd, and I wouldn't know anyone at this party other than him and Alexis. And Jared now, but he was dangerous to be around.

"At least stop by for a few minutes," Jared said, giving me that warm smile again. I practically melted all over the floor, like a chocolate left in the sun. So unfair.

Alexis glanced between me and Jared with an amused smile, like she could tell how he affected me. "Yes, you have to come."

Kyle nudged me with his elbow. "C'mon. You can check out our studio while you're there."

Well…. I supposed it wasn't that late yet, and I *had* been dying to check out the band's studio. It would be a good friend-gesture if I made an appearance, and if the party was crowded, I'd probably be able to avoid Jared the entire time. A few minutes couldn't hurt, right?

ACKNOWLEDGEMENTS

A thousand thanks to the following people, without whom I couldn't have written or published this book:

My amazing husband, Gary.

My entire family, for their endless support.

The authors who critiqued this book: Karen Akins, Riley Edgewood, Stephanie Garber, Jessica Love, Kathryn Rose, and Rachel Searles.

My agent, Kate Schafer Testerman.

My cover designer, Najla Qamber, and my photographer, Lindee Robinson.

My copy editor, Rebecca Weston.

And all the fans who loved Kyle and wanted a story about him. I hope you enjoyed the result!

ABOUT THE AUTHOR

Elizabeth Briggs is a full-time geek who writes books for teens and adults. She plays the guitar, mentors at-risk teens, and volunteers with a dog rescue group. She lives in Los Angeles with her husband and a pack of small, fluffy dogs.

Visit Elizabeth online for playlists & more!
www.elizabethbriggs.net
Facebook.com/ElizabethBriggsAuthor
Twitter: @lizwrites

19435410R00082

Made in the USA
Middletown, DE
19 April 2015